"I'll take you to meet a few people."

Katherine cringed inwardly, knowing just how plain her bargain dress must look.

"I do like that dress." The doctor smiled down at her, his eyes twinkling. "I thought you might have doubts about coming tonight, but there has to be a beginning—a first step, as it were."

She stared at him in his elegant dinner jacket. His face was pleasantly calm but, she thought, tired. "Toward what?" she wanted to know.

"Why, love, marriage, children—a lifetime of happiness."

"You really believe that?" Katherine asked. When he nodded, she said gravely, "I do, too, but sometimes it's best not to take the step."

Romance readers around the world will be saddened to note the passing of **Betty Neels** this past June. Her career spanned thirty years and she continued to write into her ninetieth year. To her millions of fans, Betty epitomized the romance writer, and yet she began writing almost by accident. She had retired from nursing, but her inquiring mind sought stimulation. Her new career was born when she heard a lady in Amsterdam bemoaning the lack of good romance novels. Betty's first book, *Sister Peters in Amsterdam*, was published in 1969, and she eventually completed 134 books. She was a wonderful person as well as a hugely talented writer, and she will be greatly missed. Her spirit will live on in all her works, including those soon to be published.

THE BEST *of*

BETTY NEELS

WHEN TWO PATHS MEET

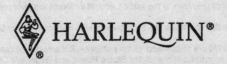

TORONTO • NEW YORK • LONDON
AMSTERDAM • PARIS • SYDNEY • HAMBURG
STOCKHOLM • ATHENS • TOKYO • MILAN • MADRID
PRAGUE • WARSAW • BUDAPEST • AUCKLAND

ISBN 0-373-51164-7

WHEN TWO PATHS MEET

First North American Publication 2001

Copyright © 1988 by Betty Neels.

This edition published by arrangement with Harlequin Books S.A.

® and TM are trademarks of the publisher. Trademarks indicated with
® are registered in the United States Patent and Trademark Office, the
Canadian Trade Marks Office and in other countries.

Visit us at www.eHarlequin.com

Printed in U.S.A.

CHAPTER ONE

KATHERINE rolled over in bed and pulled the blankets over her ears; it wasn't time to get up, she was sure of that, and she resented whatever it was that had awakened her. She tucked her cold feet into her nightie and closed her eyes, only to open them immediately at the steady thumping on the front door below her window. The milkman? Unreasonably early. A tramp? A would-be thief? But he wouldn't want to draw attention to himself.

She got out of bed, thrust her feet into slippers and dragged on her dressing-gown. By the light of her bedside lamp the alarm clock showed well past five in the morning. The thump came again, and she went softly along the landing and down the stairs; her brother and his wife, who slept at the back of the house, and very soundly too, wouldn't have heard it—nor, with luck, would the two children in the room next to her own.

It took a few moments to open the door, and she left it prudently on the chain, to peer through the narrow opening at the man on the doorstep. It was the tail end of October, and only just beginning to get light, but she could make out what appeared to be a giant.

He spoke from somewhere above her head. 'Good girl. Let me in quickly.'

He had a deep, unhurried voice which reassured her, nevertheless she asked, 'Why?'

'I have a new-born baby here, likely to die of exposure unless it gets warmed up pretty quickly.'

She undid the chain without wasting words, and he went past her. 'Where's the kitchen, or somewhere warm?'

'The end door.' She waved a hand, and applied herself to locking and bolting the door once more. All at once, she reflected that she could have bolted herself in with an escaped convict, a thief, even a murderer. And it was too late to do anything about it; she hurried him along and opened the kitchen door on to the lingering warmth of the old-fashioned Rayburn. He brushed past her, laid the bundle he was carrying on the kitchen table and unfolded it carefully and, from the depths of his car coat, exposed a very small, very quiet baby. Katherine took one look and went to poke up the fire, quietly, so as not to arouse the household.

When the man said, 'Blankets? Something warm?' she went like a small shadow back upstairs to her room and took the sheet and a blanket off her bed. The linen cupboard was on the landing outside her brother's room, and he or Joyce might hear the door squeaking.

She handed them to the man, who took them without looking at her, only muttering, 'Sensible girl,' and then, 'Warm water?'

There was always a large kettle keeping warm on the Rayburn; she filled a small basin and put it on the table. 'Now, just stay here for a moment, will you? I'll go to the car and get my bag.'

'I've locked the door, and my brother might hear if you go through the back door, it creaks. I'll have to go and unlock...'

He was looking around him; the house was old-fashioned, and the kitchen windows were large and sashed. He crossed the room and silently slid one open, climbed through soundlessly and disappeared, to reappear just as silently very shortly after. He was a very large man indeed, which made his performance all the more impressive. Katherine, who had picked up the blanketed baby and was holding it close, stared at him over the woolly folds.

'You are indeed a sensible girl,' observed the man, and put his bag down on the table. 'This little fellow needs a bit of tidying up...'

It was a relief to Katherine to see a little colour stealing through the scrap on the table. She handed the things he asked for from his bag and whispered, 'Will he be all right?'

'I think so, babies are extremely tough; it rather depends on how long he's been lying on the side of the road.'

'How could anyone...?' She stared across the table at him, seeing him properly for the first time. He was a handsome man, with fair hair and sleepy blue eyes under straight brows, and above a wide, firm mouth his nose was pure aquiline. Katherine was aware of a strange sensation somewhere under her ribs, a kind of delightful breathlessness, a splendid warmth and a tingling. She stayed quite still, a small, rather thin girl, with an ordinary face which was redeemed from plainness by a pair of beautiful grey eyes, heavily fringed with black lashes. Her hair, alas, was a pale, soft brown, straight and long. Wrapped as she was in the useful, dark red dressing-gown Joyce, her sister-in-law, had given her the previous Christmas, she presented a picture of complete mediocrity. Which made it entirely unsuitable that she should have fallen in love with a man who was looking at her kindly enough, but with no hint of interest in her person.

She said in her quiet voice, 'Would you like a cup of tea? And where will you take the baby?'

'To hospital, as quickly as possible…' He paused, looking over her shoulder, and she turned round. Joyce was in the doorway.

She was a handsome young woman, but now her good looks were spoilt by the look of amazed rage on her face.

'Katherine—what on earth is the meaning of this? And who is this man? Have you taken leave of your senses?'

'If I might explain?' The man's voice was quiet, but something in it made Joyce silent. 'I found a new-born child on the roadside—this house was only a few yards away, I knocked for help. This young lady has most kindly and efficiently provided it. May I trespass on your kindness still further, and ask her to come with me to the hospital so that she may hold the baby?'

Joyce had had time to study him, and her manner changed rapidly. She tossed a long curl over her shoulder, and pulled her quilted dressing-gown rather more tightly around her splendid figure. If Katherine had looked ordinary before, she was now completely overshadowed. Joyce ignored her.

'You're a doctor? I must say all this is very unusual. I'll make you a hot drink. You must be so tired.' She smiled charmingly at him and said sharply to Katherine, 'You heard what the doctor said, Katherine. Don't just stand there, go and get dressed.'

And, when she had slipped away without looking at anyone, 'My husband's young sister—she lives with us.' She gave a tinkling little laugh. 'Not ideal, of course, but one has certain responsibilities. Now, what about that drink? I don't know your name…'

'I'll not stop for anything, thank you, Mrs…'

'Marsh—Joyce Marsh.'

He was bending over the baby again. 'I'll see that your sister-in-law gets back safely.' He straightened himself to his full height. 'Please make my apologies to your husband. Ah, here is Miss Marsh.'

Katherine, very neat in slacks and a short jacket, her hair screwed into a bun, came into the room. Without a word, she held out her arms for the baby, waited while the doctor picked up his coat and bag and bade a courteous goodbye to Joyce, and then followed him down the passage, with Joyce trailing behind. She made rather a thing of unbolting the door.

'I'm not very strong,' she murmured. 'So sorry, and having to get out of my bed at such an unearthly hour.' She gave her little tinkling laugh again.

'Wait here,' the doctor bade Katherine. 'I'll get the car.' He went down the short path to the gate.

It was very quiet and his hearing was excellent, so he couldn't fail to hear Joyce's sharp, 'Just you get back here without wasting any time. I'm not seeing to the children; they'll have to stay in bed until you're here to get them up.'

The morning light was strengthening; the car outside the gate looked large. The doctor got out and took the baby from Katherine, bade Joyce a coldly courteous goodbye, and opened the car door. Katherine got in, took the baby on to her lap, and sat without speaking while he got in beside her. She was a little surprised when he picked up the phone and had a brief conversation with someone—the hospital, she supposed. She had heard of phones in cars, but she had never seen one, only on television.

He drove in silence, a little too fast for her liking, along the narrow road which brought them to the main road in Salisbury. The early morning heavy traffic was building up, but he drove steadily and fast, circumventing the city until he reached the roundabout on its outskirts and took the road to the hospital.

They were expected. He drew up smoothly before the accident centre entrance, opened Katherine's door and urged her through into the hospital. The baby was taken from her at once by a tired-looking night sister, and carried away with the doctor, a young houseman in a white coat, and another nurse behind them. Katherine watched them go and, since there was no one to ask where she should go, she sat herself down on one of the benches ranged around the walls. She would have liked a cup of tea, breakfast would have been even better, but she was a sensible girl, there were other more pressing matters to see to. She suspected that she had already been forgotten.

But she hadn't; within ten minutes or so she was approached by a young nurse. 'Dr Fitzroy says you're to have breakfast. I'll take you along to the canteen and you are to wait there when you have had it—he'll join you later.'

'I have to get back home...' began Katherine, her thoughts wincing away from Joyce's wrath if she didn't.

'Dr Fitzroy says he'll take you back, and you are please to do as he asks.'

The nurse so obviously expected her to do so, that Katherine got to her feet, mentally consigning Joyce and the children to a later hour, when she could worry about them at her leisure. For the moment, she was hungry.

The canteen was empty; it was too soon for the night staff going off duty, too early for the day staff, even now getting out of their beds. The nurse sat Katherine down at one of the plastic-covered tables and went over to the counter. She came back with a loaded tray: cornflakes, eggs and bacon, toast, butter and marmalade, and a pot of tea.

'I haven't any money with me,' Katherine pointed out anxiously.

'Dr Fitzroy said you were to have a good breakfast. I don't think he meant you to pay for it.' The nurse smiled and said goodbye and disappeared.

Katherine's small nose sniffed at the fragrant aroma rising from the tray. To have breakfast served to her, and such a breakfast, was a treat not to be missed. And she applied herself to the cornflakes without further ado.

She ate everything, and was emptying the teapot when Dr Fitzroy joined her.

She smiled up at him. 'Thank you for my breakfast,' she said in her quiet, sensible way. 'Is there no way I can get back without you bothering to take me?'

At the sight of him, her heart had started thumping against her ribs, but she looked much as usual—rather a nonentity of a girl, badly dressed and too thin. Dr Fitzroy sat down opposite her; a kind man, he felt sorry for her, although he wasn't sure why. He hadn't been taken in by her sister-in-law's gushing manner. Probably the girl had a dull life, as well as having to live with a woman who obviously didn't like her overmuch.

He said kindly, 'If you're ready, I'll drive you back and make my excuses to your sister-in-law. They will be wondering where you are.'

Katherine got to her feet at once; the pleasant little adventure was over and she would be made to pay for it, she had no doubt of that. But it would be worth it. Joyce's spite and her brother's indifference wouldn't be able to spoil it. It was ridiculous to fall in love as she had done; she had had no idea that she could feel so deeply about anyone. It would be a dream she would have to keep to herself for the rest of her life; it hadn't the remotest chance of ever being more than that. She buttoned her jacket and went with him through the hospital and out to the forecourt where the car was standing.

'Is the baby all right?' she asked as he drove away.

'Yes, although it's rather early days to know for certain that he's taken no harm. A nice little chap.'

She shivered. 'If you hadn't seen him and stopped…'

'We must try and find the mother.' He glanced sideways at her. 'I hope I haven't disrupted your morning too much.'

She said, 'Oh, no,' much too quickly, so that he looked at her for a second time, but her face was quite calm.

All the same, when they reached the house he said, 'I'll come in with you.'

She had her hand on the car door. 'Oh, really, there's no need, you must be busy…'

He took no notice, but got out of the car and went round to her door. He opened it for her and they walked up the path to the side door. 'We don't use the front door much,' she explained matter-of-factly. 'It makes a lot of extra work.'

She opened the side door on to a flagstoned passage, and prayed silently that he would go before

Joyce discovered that she was back home. Prayers aren't always answered—Joyce's voice, strident with ill temper, came from an open door at the end of the passage.

'So you're back, and high time, too! You can go straight upstairs and see to the children, and if you think you're going to have your breakfast first, you are very much mistaken.' The door flung wide open and Joyce appeared. 'You little…' She stopped short. The change in her manner was ludicrous as she caught sight of the doctor behind Katherine.

'There you are, dear.' She smiled widely as she spoke, 'Do run upstairs and see if the children are ready, will you? I've been so busy.'

Katherine didn't say anything to this, but held out her hand to the doctor. It was engulfed in a firm grasp which was very comforting, and just for a moment she wanted to weep because she wouldn't see him again, only be left with a delightful dream.

'Thank you for bringing me back, and for my breakfast, Dr Fitzroy. I hope the little baby will find someone to love him.'

He looked down at her gravely. 'It is I who thank you, Miss Marsh. Your help undoubtedly helped to save his life. Be sure we shall try and find his mother, and if not, get him adopted.'

She looked up into his face, learning it by heart, for the memory of it was all she would have of him. 'Goodbye,' she said, as she went away, past Joyce, into the hall and up the stairs to where Robin and Sarah could be heard wailing and shouting.

They were unlovable children, largely because their mother had no patience with them, and their father, a schoolmaster, had no time for them. They had been thrust into Katherine's care when she had gone to live with her brother two years ago, after her mother died, with the frequently expressed opinion on his part that, since he was giving her a home, she might as well keep herself occupied by looking after the children. It was something she had been unable to dispute, for she had left school to nurse her mother, and when she died she had been glad to go to her brother's home. She had been nineteen then, with vague ideas about training for a job and being independent, but now, two years later, without money and with very little time to herself, she was no nearer that. She had made several efforts to leave his house, but somehow she never managed it. The children fell ill with measles, or Joyce took to her bed, declaring that she was too ill to be left. On her last attempt, her brother had reminded her in his cold way that she owed everything to him, and the least she could do was to remain with the children until they were old enough to go to school. Almost two years still to go, she reflected, opening the nursery door on to a scene of chaos. The pair of them had got out of their beds, and were running round, flinging anything they could lay their hands on at each other.

Katherine suppressed a sigh. 'Hello, dears. Who's going to get dressed? And what would you like for breakfast?'

They had wet their beds, so she stripped the bedclothes off, caught the children in turn and took off their sopping nightclothes, then bathed and dressed them. Shutting the door on the muddle she would have to sort out presently, she took them down to the kitchen.

Joyce was in the hall, pulling on her gloves. 'I'm going to the hairdressers. If I'm not back, get lunch, will you? Oh, and take them out for a walk.'

The day was like all her other days: Robin and Sarah to feed and care for, unending ironing and the washing machine in everlasting use, beds to make, the nursery to keep tidy. She went steadily ahead with her chores; she was a girl with plenty of common sense, and months earlier she had realised that self-pity got her nowhere. She was fed and clothed, albeit as cheaply as possible, and she had a roof over her head. Unemployment, her brother had reminded her on a number of occasions, was high; she had no chance of getting a job, not even an unskilled one. When she had protested that she could train as a typist, or get a job in some domestic capacity, he had told her that the chance of a job for a newly qualified typist would be slender, and the training a complete waste of money. And, as for domestic work, what was she thinking of? No sister of his was going to be anyone's servant!

'But I would at least get paid,' she had told him with quiet persistence, in consequence of which he hadn't spoken to her for several days.

Apart from her lack of money, and the heavy-handed persuasion of her brother, Katherine couldn't bring herself to leave because of the children. They had no affection for her, nor she for them, but she was sorry for them. Other than herself, no one bothered much about them. Joyce was out a great deal, sitting on a variety of committees in the cause of charity, leaving the running of the house to Katherine and the spasmodic assistance of Mrs Todd from the farm cottages down the road, who came each day to dust and vacuum and, occasionally, when she felt like it, to polish the furniture or wash the flagstone floors in the hall and kitchen. She was a bad-tempered woman, and she disliked the children, so Katherine did her best to keep them out of her way.

In the afternoon, Mrs Todd had signified her intention of washing the kitchen floor, provided those dratted children were out of the way, so Katherine prudently dressed them warmly and took them for a walk. Sarah was still too small to walk far; it meant taking the pushchair and, since Robin declared that he was tired, she pushed them both back from the village, thankful to find when they got in that Mrs Todd had gone, leaving a tolerably clean kitchen and a terse note, reminding Joyce that she was owed two weeks' wages. Katherine left the note where it was, got the children's tea and, since there was no sign of Joyce, began to make preparations for the evening meal. Joyce came back just as she was finished with cleaning the vegetables, slammed a parcel down on the kitchen table, said, 'Sausages,' and turned to go out of the kitchen again.

'There's a note from Mrs Todd,' Katherine pointed

out, 'and it's either sausages or children—which do you want t> do?'

Joyce cast her a look of dislike. 'I have never met such an ungrateful, lazy girl—' she began and caught Katherine's mildly surprised eyes. 'Oh, I'll cook the supper, I suppose, since there's no one else. Really, too much is expected of me! Here am I, busy all day with Oxfam and Save the Children and that jumble sale for the primary school, and you've been at home, doing nothing...'

Katherine let that pass; she had heard the same thing on any number of occasions. She collected the children and bore them off to their baths. While she got them ready for their beds, she thought about Dr Fitzroy. He would be married, of course, to a pretty wife, and there would be children, well-behaved, loving children, and they would live in one of those nice old houses close to the cathedral in Salisbury. Pure envy shot through her at the thought, and was instantly stifled.

Robin, being dried, kicked her shins and ran out of the bathroom. Unfortunately, he ran straight into his father's path as he was on his way to his room to freshen up for the evening. The boy was led howling back to the bathroom.

'Really, Katherine, you must control the children! This is surely proof that you are quite unsuitable for any kind of responsible job. I can only hope that you will learn something from us while you are living here.'

She was wrestling a nightie over Sarah's head and

didn't look up. 'Don't be pompous,' she begged him, 'and don't talk nonsense. And I've learnt a good deal while I've been living here, you know. How to manage without help from either you or Joyce, how to live without so much as a tenpenny piece to call my own...' She spoke quietly because she was a quiet girl, but inside she was boiling with frustration. She added kindly, 'Don't gobble like that, Henry. It's no good getting in a rage. I do my best, but I'm beginning to wonder why.'

She went past him with a squirming Sarah in her arms, intending to tuck her up in her cot and to go back for Robin, who was bawling his head off.

Supper was by no means a pleasant meal: Joyce, sulking because Henry had been sarcastic about burnt sausages and not quite cooked potatoes, had little to say, while he delivered a few well-chosen words about his day's work, the pursuit of which had left him, he said, drained of energy. From this, he hinted strongly that the effort to keep his household in comfort was almost too much for him.

Here, Joyce interrupted him in a cross voice. Did he forget, she wanted to know, how hard *she* worked, getting to know the right people for his benefit? Did he realise how her day was entirely taken up with meeting boring women on committees?

Katherine, sitting between them, ate her sausages because she was hungry, and said nothing at all. Indeed, she wasn't really listening, she was thinking about Dr Fitzroy, a small luxury she hugged to herself. She had embarked on a pleasant daydream where she fell and sprained an ankle and was taken to hospital, there to find him waiting to treat it while he expressed delight and pleasure at meeting her again...

'Katherine, I wish that you would attend when I speak to you.' Henry's voice snapped the dream in two, and she blinked at him, reluctant to return to her present surroundings.

'I feel that it's time for Robin to start simple lessons. There is no reason why you shouldn't spend an hour with him each morning, teaching him his letters and simple figures.'

'What a good idea,' she agreed cheerfully. 'He's quite out of hand, you know, because he hasn't enough to occupy his brain. What will Sarah do while I'm busy with Robin?'

'Why, she can stay in the room with you.'

'Out of the question.' She was still cheerful. 'He wouldn't listen to a word. Perhaps Joyce could spare an hour?'

Her sister-in-law pushed back her chair. 'Whatever next? Where am I to find an hour, even half an hour? You can argue it out between you.'

'The thing to do,' observed Katherine mildly, 'would be to take him with you when you go to work, and drop him off at that playschool in Wilton. He needs other children, you know. Perhaps Joyce could take her car and collect him at lunch time?' She felt Henry's fulminating eye upon her, and added calmly, 'I'm sure several children from the village go there. I dare say they would give Robin a lift?'

She took no notice of his shocked silence, but began to clear the table. Mrs Todd strongly objected to washing the supper dishes when she arrived in the morning.

The subject of Robin's education didn't crop up again for several days. Indeed, Henry showed his displeasure at Katherine's lack of co-operation by saying as few words to her as possible, something she didn't mind in the least. As for Joyce, they met at meals, but very seldom otherwise. Katherine, her days full of unending chores, had no time to worry about that. In bed, in the peace and quiet of her room, she strengthened her resolve to find a job of some sort. Lack of money was the stumbling point, and she hadn't found a way round that yet, but she would. She promised herself that each night, before allowing her thoughts to dwell on Dr Fitzroy. It was a pity that she was too tired to indulge in this for more than a minute or two.

She was in the kitchen, washing up the supper dishes, more than a week since she had answered the knock on the door which had so changed her feelings, when Henry's voice, loud and demanding, caused her to put down the dishmop and hurry along the passage to the drawing-room. One of the children, she supposed, not bothering to take off her apron; they had been almost unmanageable all day, and were probably wrecking the nursery instead of going to sleep. She opened the door and put her untidy head round it.

'I'm washing up,' she began. 'If it's the children...'

Dr Fitzroy was standing in the middle of the room, while Henry stood with his back to the fireplace, looking uneasy, and Joyce sat at a becoming angle in her chair, showing a good deal of leg.

'Dr Fitzroy wishes to speak to you, Katherine.' Henry was at his most ponderous.

'Hello,' said the doctor, and smiled at her.

Her face lit up with delight. 'Oh, hello,' said Katherine. 'How very nice to see you again!'

She had come into the room, and stood unselfconsciously in front of him. That she was a deplorable sight hadn't entered her head; it was stuffed with bliss at the mere sight of him.

'What about the baby? Is he all right?'

'Splendid. Perhaps we might go somewhere and talk?' He looked at Henry, who went puce with temper.

'Anything you have to say to Katherine can surely be listened to by myself and my wife? I am her brother,' he blustered.

'Yes, I know.' The doctor's voice was silky. He didn't say any more, so Henry was forced to speak.

'There is the dining-room, although I can't imagine what you can have to say to Katherine...'

'No, I don't suppose you can.' Dr Fitzroy's voice was as pleasant as his smile. He held the door open, and Katherine went past him to the dining-room. It was chilly there; she switched on the light and turned to look at him.

Just for a moment he had a pang of doubt. What had made him think that this shabby, small young woman would be just right for the job he had in mind? But, even if he had had second thoughts, the

eager face she had turned to him doused them at once.
She had shown admirable common sense about the
baby; she hadn't bothered him with a lot of questions,
nor had she complained once. And, from what he had
just seen, life at home was something she wasn't
likely to miss.

'Do sit down. I'm sorry it's chilly in here.'

She sat composedly, her hands quiet in her lap, and
waited for him to speak.

'I have a job to offer you,' he began without pre-
amble. 'Of course, you may not want one, but I believe that you are exactly right for the kind of work
I have in mind.' He paused and studied her face; it
had become animated and a little pink, but she didn't
speak. 'I have been attending two elderly patients for
some years, and they have reached the age when they
need someone to look after them. They have help in
the house, so there would be no housework...' His
eyes dwelt for a moment on her apron. 'They refuse
to have a nurse—in fact, they don't really need one.
What they do need is someone to fetch and carry, find
their spectacles, encourage them to eat their meals,
accompany them in the car when they wish to go out,
and see them safely to their beds, and, if necessary,
go to them during the night. In short, an unobtrusive
companion, ready to fall in with their wishes and keep
an eye on them. I've painted rather a drab picture, but
it has its bright side—the house is pleasant and there
is a delightful garden. You will have time for yourself
each day and be independent. The salary is forty
pounds a week...'

'Forty pounds? A week? I've never had...' She stopped just in time from telling him that she seldom had more than forty pence in her pocket. He wouldn't believe her if she did. She finished rather lamely, 'A job, I'm not trained for anything, Henry says...'

'Perhaps you will allow me to be the judge of that?' he suggested kindly. 'Will it be difficult for you to leave home?'

She thought for a moment. 'Yes, but I'm twenty-one. Would you mind very much if I told them now, while you are here?'

'Certainly I will stay. Perhaps if there is any difficulty, I may be able to persuade your brother. When could you come with me to see Mr and Mrs Grainger?'

She resisted the wish to shout 'Now!' and said in her matter-of-fact way, 'Whenever you wish, Dr Fitzroy.'

'I'll come for you tomorrow morning, and if you and they like each other, perhaps you could start on the following day?'

Katherine closed her eyes for a moment. There would be angry words and bad temper and endless arguments, but they couldn't last for ever. 'I'd like that.'

She got up, went to the door and found him there, pushing it open for her, something Henry had never done for her; good manners weren't to be wasted on a sister that he didn't particularly like. He was still standing before the fireplace and, from the way that he and Joyce looked at her as she went in, she knew that they had been talking about her. She crossed the room and stood in front of her brother.

'Dr Fitzroy has offered me a job, which I have accepted,' she told him in a voice which she was glad to hear sounded firm.

Henry gobbled, 'A job? What kind of job, pray? And what about the children?'

She said calmly, 'I should think you could get a mother's help—after all, most people do—or Joyce could give up some of her committees.' She sighed because Henry was working himself into a rage, and Joyce, once the doctor had gone, would be even worse.

Dr Fitzroy spoke now in a slow, placid manner which disregarded Henry's red face. 'Your sister is exactly right for an excellent post with two of my elderly patients. I have been searching for someone for some time, and her good sense when I asked for her help the other morning convinced me that she is exactly what Mr and Mrs Grainger need. I shall call for her in the morning so that she may have an interview, and I hope she will be able to go to them on the following day.'

Joyce said shrilly, 'Who are these people? We know nothing about them! Katherine has never been away from home before; she'll miss home life...' She caught the doctor's sardonic eye and paused. 'She can go now, as far as I'm concerned,' she said sulkily.

He ignored her. 'I'll be here at nine o'clock, if that suits you?' He had spoken to Katherine, and then turned to Henry. 'You may have my word that your sister will be happy as companion to the Graingers. There will be no housework, of course, and she will be paid a salary.' He added a very civil goodnight, and Katherine, walking on air, took him to the door.

Before she shut it, he asked, 'You'll be all right?'

She nodded; there would be a good deal of unpleasantness before she could go to her room and start packing and looking out something suitable to wear in the morning, but she felt capable of outfacing the forthcoming recriminations with the promise of such a splendid future before her. And she would see Dr Fitzroy, too, sometimes. She hugged the thought to herself as she went back to the drawing-room.

CHAPTER TWO

IT WAS a good thing that Katherine felt so euphoric about her future, for the next hour tried her sorely. Henry, having recovered from his first surprise, had marshalled a number of forceful arguments, hampered rather than helped by Joyce's ill-natured complaints.

Katherine listened patiently and, when he had quite done, said kindly, 'Well, Henry, I would have thought that you would have been pleased. You don't need to be responsible for me any more, do you?'

Henry was an alarming puce once more. 'Your ingratitude cuts me to the quick,' he told her. 'After all this time, giving you a home and food and clothes…'

She smiled at him and said sensibly, 'And look what you got for that—unpaid housework, someone to look after the children and, because I'm your sister, there was no need to give me an allowance.' She added, 'It will be nice to have some money.' Emboldened by the prospect of a glowing future, she walked to the door, just as Henry got his breath for another speech. 'I'm rather tired,' she said matter-of-factly. 'I think I'll go to bed. I haven't finished the washing up, but there are only the saucepans left to do. Goodnight, Joyce—Henry.'

In her room, she sat down on her bed and cried.

She had tried hard to please Henry and Joyce, she had accepted the care of the children and she had done her best to love them, but it was a singularly unloving household. She had never been happy in it and she was glad to leave it. All the same, it would have been nice if Henry and Joyce had uttered just one word of encouragement or thanks.

She got up presently, and crossed the landing to the children's room. They needed tucking up once more, and she did this with her usual care, before going to the boxroom and fetching her two cases. Packing wouldn't take long: her wardrobe was small, and most of it wasn't worth packing. She had a tweed suit, elderly but well cut and good material; she would have to wear that until she had enough money to buy some decent clothes. She hoped that Mr and Mrs Grainger weren't the kind of people to dress for dinner; it seemed unlikely, but she had a plain wool dress, very out-of-date, like the suit, but it had at one time been good, and would pass muster at a pinch.

She felt better now she had started her packing. She got ready for bed, hopped between the chilly sheets, closed her eyes and, very much to her surprise, went to sleep at once.

It was a scramble in the morning. Katherine got up earlier than usual, got into the suit and the sensible, low-heeled shoes which were suitable for everyday wear and country walks with the children. Then she did her face carefully with the sketchy make-up she possessed, tied her hair back with a narrow ribbon and went along to the nursery. For once, good fortune was on her side; the children were quite willing to be washed and dressed and given their breakfast. She took them downstairs and made tea for herself, laid the table for the children and for Henry, who wouldn't be down for half an hour or so, and gave them their breakfast. She was too excited to eat, and she hadn't considered what meals they would have later on. She wasn't even sure when she would be back; what was more, she didn't much care!

She cleared the table, took the children to the play-room and made more tea for Henry, who, on his way downstairs, put his head round the door to wish the children good morning but ignored her. She heard him leave the house presently and Mrs Todd crashing plates and saucepans in the kitchen. She would have to get Joyce out of bed before she went. Dr Fitzroy had said nine o'clock, and it was ten minutes to the hour.

Joyce didn't answer as she went into the bedroom. Katherine drew back the curtains. 'I'm going now,' she said. 'The children have had their breakfast and are in the playroom. I don't know when I'll be back.'

Joyce lifted her head. 'I feel ill,' she said pettishly. 'You simply can't go—you'll have to put this inter-view off until I'm better.'

Katherine took a look at her sister-in-law. 'I'll tell Mrs Todd. I dare say she'll keep an eye on Sarah and Robin. Henry can always come back here—you could phone him.'

Joyce sat right up. 'I hope these people hate you

on sight and you lose the job. It would serve you right! And don't expect to come crawling back here. Job or no job, out you go tomorrow.'

Katherine turned to go, and the children, bored with their own company, came hurtling past her and flung themselves onto their mother's bed.

Katherine closed the door quietly behind her. She didn't like her sister-in-law, but a pang of sympathy shot through her; the children were small tyrants, and Joyce had little patience with them. She would demand a mother's help and Henry would have to agree. Whoever it was would want a salary and days off and weekends and holidays...Katherine had another pang of sympathy for Henry, who hated to spend his money.

Dr Fitzroy was waiting for her when she opened the door and looked out, and she hurried to the car.

'Good morning.' She was a bit breathless with an upsurge of feeling at the sight of him. 'I hope you haven't been waiting.'

'Just got here. Jump in.' He held the door for her, and she settled in the seat beside him. 'Nervous?' he asked. 'You needn't be.'

He gave her a reassuring smile, and thought what a dim little thing she was in her out-of-date suit and sturdy shoes. But sensible and quiet, just what the Graingers needed, and they would hardly notice what she was wearing, only that her voice was pleasant and she was calm in a crisis. He started the car. 'I'll tell you something about Mr and Mrs Grainger. In their seventies, almost eighty, in fact. He has a heart condition and is far too active, can be peppery if he can't have his own way. Mrs Grainger is small and meek and perfectly content to allow him to dictate to her. She has arthritis and suffers a good deal of pain, but never complains. They are devoted to each other. They lost their only son in an accident some years ago, but they have a granddaughter...'

Something in his voice caught Katherine's attention; this granddaughter was someone special to him. She had known from the moment she knew that she had fallen in love with him that he would never look at her—all the same, it was a blow. So silly, she told herself silently, he could have been married already, with a houseful of children. At the back of her head, a small, defiant voice pointed out that he might have been heart-whole and single and miraculously bowled over by her very ordinary person. She became aware that he had asked her something and she hadn't been heeding.

'So sorry,' she said quickly. 'You asked me something?'

They were at the roundabout on the outskirts of Wilton, waiting to find a place in the traffic streaming towards Salisbury. He slipped smoothly between two other cars before he answered. 'You do understand that there will be no regular hours? You will, of course, have time to yourself each day, but that time may vary. It would be difficult to arrange to meet your friends or make dates.'

She said quietly, in a bleak little voice, 'I haven't any friends, and no one to make a date with.' She added quickly, in case he thought she was wallowing in self-pity, 'I had lots of friends when my mother was alive, but there wasn't much time to spare at my brother's house. I—I like to be busy, and I shan't mind at all if Mr and Mrs Grainger make their own arrangements about my free time.'

'That's settled then.' He sounded kind but faintly uninterested. 'But I expect you will want to go shopping.' He was annoyed that he had said that, for she went pink and turned to look out of her window, very conscious of her dull appearance. All the same, she agreed cheerfully; in a week or two she would indeed go shopping. Clothes made the man, it was said— well, they would make her, too!

She liked Salisbury; the cathedral dominated the city, and its close was a delightful oasis in the city centre. When the doctor drove down High Street and through the great gate, circled the small car park and drew up before one of the charming old houses abutting the close, she declared, 'Oh, is it here? I've always wanted...I came here with Mother...'

'Charming, isn't it? And yes, this is the house.' He got out and went round to open her door. They crossed the pavement together, and he rang the bell beside the pedimented doorway. The door was opened almost at once by a middle-aged woman with a stern face, dressed soberly in black. She gave the doctor a wintry smile and stared at Katherine.

'Ah, Mrs Dowling, I have brought Miss Marsh to meet Mr and Mrs Grainger. They are expecting us.'

She wished him a reluctant good morning and nodded at Katherine, who smiled uncertainly. 'You'd better come up,' she observed dourly.

The house, despite its Georgian façade, was considerably older. A number of passages led off the small, square hall, and half a dozen steps at its end ended in a small gallery with two doors. The housekeeper opened one of them and ushered them inside. The room was large and long, at the back of the house, overlooking a surprisingly large garden.

Its two occupants turned to look at the doctor and Katherine as they went in, and the elderly gentleman said at once, 'Jason, my dear boy—so here you are with the little lady you have found for us.' He peered over his glasses at Katherine. 'Good morning, my dear. You don't find it too irksome to cherish us, I hope?'

'How do you do, Mr Grainger?' said Katherine politely. 'Not in the least, if you would like me to come.'

'Take a look at her, my dear,' begged the old gentleman, addressing himself to the equally elderly lady sitting opposite him.

She was small and frail-looking, but her eyes were bright and her voice surprisingly strong. She studied Katherine and nodded. 'I believe that she will do very nicely, Albert. A little on the small side, perhaps?'

'I'm very strong,' declared Katherine on a faintly apprehensive note.

'And competent,' put in the doctor in his calm way. 'Besides not being wishful to dash off to the discos with a different young man each evening.'

He had pulled a chair forward, and nodded to her to sit down, and Mrs Grainger asked, 'Have you a young man, my dear?'

'No,' said Katherine, 'and I've never been inside a disco.'

The old couple nodded to each other. 'Most suitable. Will you come at once?'

Katherine looked at the doctor, who said placidly, 'I'll take her back to her brother's house now, and she can pack her things. I dare say, if you wish it, she could be ready to come back here this evening.'

'Oh, yes,' said Katherine, 'there's a bus I could catch...'

'I'll pick you up at six o'clock.' He barely glanced at her. 'Mrs Grainger, you do understand that Miss Marsh has to have an hour or so to herself each day, and at least a half-day off each week? We have already discussed the salary, and she finds it acceptable.' He got up. 'I'm going to have a word with Mrs Dowling, if I may, before I take Miss Marsh back.'

He was gone for ten minutes, during which time Katherine was plied with questions. She answered them readily enough, for she liked her employers.

She was sensible enough to realise that sitting here in this pleasant room wasn't indicative of her day's work; she would probably be on the run for a good part of each day and probably the night, too, but after the cheerless atmosphere of Henry's home this delightful house held warmth, something she had missed since her mother had died.

When Dr Fitzroy returned, she rose, shook hands,

declared that she would return that evening, and accompanied the doctor out to his car.

He had little to say as they drove back, only expressed himself satisfied with the interview, warned her to be ready that evening and reminded her that he called to see Mr and Mrs Grainger two days a week, usually on Tuesdays and Fridays, at about eleven o'clock. 'So I should like you to be there when I call.' He shot her a quick glance. 'You will be happy there?'

'Yes, oh, yes!' she assured him. 'I can't believe it! I'm so afraid that I'll wake up and find that it's all been a dream.'

He laughed. 'It's true enough, and I do warn you that you may find the work irksome and sometimes tiring.' He stopped the car outside Henry's gate and got out. 'I'll come in with you and speak to your sister-in-law.'

Joyce was waiting for them in the drawing-room, beautifully turned out and, judging from the din the children were making from the nursery, impervious to their demands.

As Katherine went in with the doctor, she said, 'Katherine, do go upstairs and see to the children. I'm exhausted already—I had to sit down quietly...'

She smiled bewitchingly at the doctor, who didn't smile back. 'Mrs Marsh, Miss Marsh will be taking up her job this evening. I shall be here for her at six o'clock. I'm sure you'll make certain that she has the time to collect her things together before then.' He smiled at Katherine. 'You can be ready by then? I have an appointment in the evening and must go to the hospital this afternoon, otherwise I would come for you after lunch.'

'I'll be ready.' Katherine gave him a beaming smile. 'Thank you for taking me this morning.'

'You'll stay for coffee?' asked Joyce persuasively.

'Thank you, no.' He shook her hand and Katherine took him to the door.

'Scared?' he asked softly. 'Don't worry, if you haven't been given the chance to pack, I'll do it for you when I come.' He patted her briskly on the shoulder. 'I bless the day I knocked on this door; I've been searching for weeks for someone like you.' Her heart leapt at his words, and then plummeted to her toes as he added, 'You're exactly what the Graingers need.'

She stood for a moment or two after he had gone, dismissing sentimental nonsense from her head, preparing herself for the unpleasantness to come. And unpleasant it was, too, for Joyce was at her most vindictive.

Katherine allowed the worst of it to flow over her head and, when Joyce paused for breath, said in her calm way, 'Well, Joyce, Robin and Sarah are your children, after all. If you don't want to look after them, Henry can quite afford to get someone who will.'

She went up to her room and finished her packing which, since she had very few possessions, took no time at all. She was just finishing when Mrs Todd called up the stairs. 'Mrs Marsh 'as gone out, and them dratted kids is all over my kitchen!'

Katherine had changed back into elderly jeans and a sweater. She pulled on her jacket now and went downstairs. The children were running wild, sensing that something was happening and cheerfully adding to the disruption.

'Mrs Todd, help me cut some sandwiches and prepare a thermos—I'll take the children out and we can find somewhere to picnic. I know it's not much of a day, but it'll get them out of the house. Leave the key under the mat if we're not back, will you?'

They set out half an hour later, the children unwilling at first but, once away from the house, walking along the bridle paths, they could race about and shout as much as they wanted to. Katherine suspected that Joyce had taken herself off for the day in the hope that, if she didn't return, Katherine would feel bound to stay, but Henry would be home by five o'clock, and an hour later Dr Fitzroy would come for her.

She found a hollow out of the wind, and they ate their sandwiches there and then started back home. The children were tired now and, once they were back in the empty house, they were willing enough to have their outdoor things taken off and to settle at the kitchen table while Katherine got their tea. They had just finished when their father got home.

Katherine greeted him briskly. 'Joyce isn't back— I don't know where she went. The children have had their tea, and I've put everything ready for them to be put to bed presently.'

'What about my supper?'

'I really wouldn't know, Henry. I'm sure Joyce will have arranged something. Dr Fitzroy is coming for me at six o'clock.'

He looked aghast. 'But you can't leave us like this! Who's going to put the children to bed and get the supper?'

He had treated her as a kind of maid of all work for the last two years, but she could still feel sorry for him. 'Henry, you knew I was taking this job. You need never bother with me again, for you have never liked having me here, have you? Find a nice strong girl to help Joyce with the children, and persuade Joyce to give up some of her committees and spend more time at home.'

'I'll decide what is best, thank you, Katherine.' He was being pompous again and her concern for him faded. 'While you are waiting, you might get the children to bed.'

'They don't go until half-past six,' she pointed out. 'Why not take them to the nursery and read to them? I have a few last-minute things to do...'

She left him looking outraged.

It was five minutes to six when Joyce came home. Katherine heard her voice, loud and complaining. 'Where's Katherine? Why aren't the children with her? What about supper? I'm far too tired to do anything—she'll have to stay until tomorrow, or until someone can be found to help me...'

Leaving her room, her cases in either hand, Katherine heard her brother's voice, raised against the children's shrill voices and then, thankfully, the front door bell.

She hurried downstairs and opened the door and heaved a sigh of relief at the sight of Dr Fitzroy, large and reassuring. 'I haven't said goodbye,' she told him, rather pale at the prospect.

He took her cases from her, put them in the porch and went past her into the hall. 'I'll come with you,' he said and gave an encouraging little smile.

A waste of time as it turned out; Joyce turned her back and Henry glared at her and began a diatribe about ungrateful girls who would get what they deserved, deserting young children at a moment's notice. The doctor cut him short in the politest way. 'Fortunately, they have parents to look after them,' he observed in a bland voice which held a nasty sharp edge. 'We will be on our way.'

Katherine had said goodbye to the children, so she bade Henry and Joyce goodbye quietly and followed Dr Fitzroy out of the house, shutting the door carefully behind her. She got into the car without a word and sat silently as he drove away. It was silly to cry; she would not be missed, not as a person who had been loved, but just for a moment she felt very lonely.

The doctor said cheerfully, without looking at her, 'I often think that friends are so much better than relations, and I'm sure you'll quickly make plenty of friends.' And then he added very kindly, 'Don't cry, Katherine, they aren't worth it. You are going somewhere where you're wanted and where you'll be happy.'

She sniffed, blew her ordinary little nose and sat up straight. 'I'm sorry. You're quite right, of course. It's just that the last two years have been a complete waste of time...'

'How old are you? Twenty-one, you said? I am thirty-six, my dear, and I believe I have wasted a good many more years than two. But they are never quite wasted, you know, and all the other years make them insignificant.'

She wished with all her heart that she could stay close to his large, confident person for ever, but at least she would see him twice a week. She smiled at the thought as he said, 'That's better. Now, listen carefully. I shall only stay a few minutes at the Graingers; they dine at eight o'clock, that gives you time to find your way around and to unpack. They go to bed at ten o'clock, never later. Mrs Dowling likes her evenings to herself once she has seen to dinner, so you will get their bedtime drinks and so forth. She takes up their morning tea at half-past seven, but I don't expect she will do the same for you. It's quite a large house to run and she manages very well with two women who come in to help. Your job will be to leave her free to do that; lately she has been run off her feet, now that Mr and Mrs Grainger have become more dependent on someone to fetch and carry.'

'Does she mind me coming?'

'No, I think not, but she has been with them for twenty years or more and she is set in her ways.'

'I'll help her all I can, if she will let me. Oh, I do hope I'll make a good job of it.'

'Don't worry, you will.' They had reached Salisbury, and he was driving through the streets, quiet now after the day's traffic. Although the shops in the High Street were still lit, there were few people about, and once through North Gate it was another world, with the cathedral towering over the close and the charming old houses grouped around it at a respectable distance, as was right and proper. The doctor pulled up before the Graingers' house and got out, opened her door and collected her cases from the boot, then rang the doorbell. The door was opened so briskly that Katherine had no time to get nervous, and anyway it was too late to have cold feet. She bade Mrs Dowling a civil good evening, and accompanied the doctor to the drawing-room. Mr and Mrs Grainger were sitting on each side of a briskly burning fire, he reading a newspaper, she knitting a large woolly garment.

'There you are,' declared Mrs Grainger in a pleased voice. 'And I suppose that you must rush away, Jason? But we shall see you tomorrow, of course.' She beamed at him, and then at Katherine. 'Such a relief that you are here, my dear. Now, what shall I call you?'

'By her name, of course,' observed Mr Grainger.

'Katherine,' said Katherine.

'A very good name,' said his wife. 'I had a sister of that name—we called her Katie. She died of the scarlet fever. No one has the scarlet fever nowadays. Are you called Katie, my dear?'

'No, Mrs Grainger, although my mother always called me that.'

The old lady turned to the doctor. 'She seems a very nice girl, Jason. Not pretty, but well spoken and with a pleasant voice. I think we shall get on splendidly together.'

Mr Grainger put down his newspaper. 'Glad to have you here,' he said gruffly. 'Don't see many young faces these days, only Dodie—our granddaughter, and she has got a life of her own, bless her. You're only young once.' He glanced at Dr Fitzroy, standing placidly between them. 'Seen her lately?'

'Yes, and we're dining together this evening.'

'Then you won't want to be hanging around here with us old fogeys.'

The doctor left very shortly, and Mrs Dowling was summoned to take Katherine to her room. She was led silently up the carpeted stairs with shallow treads and along a short passage leading to the back of the house.

'Here you are,' said Mrs Dowling, rather ungraciously. 'The bathroom's beyond.' She opened a door, and Katherine went past her into a fair-sized room, prettily furnished, its window overlooking the large garden. Her cases were already there and Mrs Dowling said, 'Dinner's at eight o'clock, so you'll have time to unpack first. They won't expect you to change this evening. Mrs Grainger asked me to take you round the house. Come downstairs when you are ready and I'll do that, though it's not the easiest of times for me, what with dinner to dish up and all.'

'Would you prefer me to come with you now? I can unpack later when I come to bed, and it won't take me long to tidy myself.'

Mrs Dowling relaxed her stern expression; the girl looked harmless enough and, heaven knew, she had no looks to speak of, not like some of the pert young things these days who thought that because they had pretty faces and smart clothes, they could indulge in bad manners towards their elders and betters. She cast an eye over Katherine's sober appearance.

'Suits me, Miss…'

'Would you mind calling me Katherine?' She smiled at the older woman. 'I haven't had a job before, and Miss Marsh is a bit—well, I *am* going to work here.'

Mrs Dowling folded her arms across her chest. 'Well, I don't know, I'm sure—how would Miss Katherine do?'

'If you prefer that, Mrs Dowling.'

They toured the bedrooms, the bathroom and the small pantry off the front landing, where Katherine would be able to make hot drinks if Mr and Mrs Grainger were wakeful during the night.

'And that's often enough,' observed Mrs Dowling, 'but the doctor will have told you that.' She led the way downstairs. 'Very kind and good he is, too. Of course, him being smitten with Miss Dodie, I dare say he sees more of them than he needs to, though they're not in the best of health.'

She opened a door in the hall, and Katherine saw the dining-room: a rather gloomy apartment, heavily furnished, with a great deal of silver on the sideboard. There was a small study next to it and a charming little room opposite, used as a breakfast-room and sitting-room, its door leading to the drawing-room and with french windows opening out on to the garden at the back of the house.

'You'd best go tidy yourself,' said Mrs Dowling. 'It's almost eight o'clock, and they'll want their drinks poured. There now, you know where the drawing-room is?'

'Yes, thank you, Mrs Dowling. Do you want me to help with dinner? I could carry in the dishes for you.'

'They wouldn't like that, thanks all the same. Besides, you'll be busy enough; they ring the bell half a dozen times in an evening for me...'

'Oh, well,' said Katherine cheerfully, 'they won't need to do that now, will they? You must have been busy.'

Mrs Dowling watched her go back upstairs. Not such a bad young woman, after all, she decided. No looks, but a nice voice, and not in the least bossy.

Mr and Mrs Grainger didn't appear to have moved when Katherine went back into the drawing-room. She poured their sherry, accepted a glass for herself, and made gentle small talk until Mrs Dowling appeared to say that dinner was on the table. And from then on the evening went well. The old people liked to talk; indeed, half the time they talked at the same time, interrupting each other quite ruthlessly.

Katherine fetched their hot milky drinks from the kitchen at ten o'clock and then saw them upstairs, staying with Mrs Grainger until that lady declared that she could very easily manage for herself.

'And if I wake in the night, my dear, there's a bell in my room. Mr Grainger has one, too. I must say it's a comfort to have you here.' She bade Katherine a kind goodnight. 'We'll have a nice little talk in the morning,' she promised.

Katherine unpacked, admired her room, had a leisurely bath and thought how lovely it was to have a bathroom all to herself. She thought, too, fleetingly of Henry and Joyce, and felt guilty because she hadn't missed them or the children. I can't be a very nice person, she reflected as she curled up snugly in her bed. Not that the idea kept her awake; she slept within moments of her head touching the pillow.

Twenty-four hours later, tired though she was, she stayed awake long enough to review her day. Not too bad, she thought sleepily. The highlight of it had been the doctor's visit, although he had been impersonal in his manner towards her; all the same, he had smiled nicely at her when he left, and expressed the view that she was exactly right for the job. The old people were demanding in a nice way, but they seemed to like her, and even Mrs Dowling had unbent a little. She had had no chance to go out, or even take an hour off, but she had hardly expected that for the first day; it had been filled with undertaking the multiple small tasks the Graingers expected of her. Going upstairs to fetch a forgotten book, Katherine found time to sympathise with Mrs Dowling, who must have been dead on her feet by bedtime...

All the same, she had been happy. The house was warm, cheerful and charmingly furnished, she had a delightful room all to herself, the meals were elegantly served and the whole tempo of life slowed down. And, over and above all that, she would be paid. It was a splendid thought on which to close her eyes.

The week wound to a close. By Saturday she had found her feet, and for the last two days she had gone out while Mr and Mrs Grainger snoozed on their beds after lunch. Mrs Dowling, she discovered, liked to put her feet up after tea for an hour or so, and Katherine had offered to do any small chores for her during that time, an offer accepted rather ungraciously by that lady.

Katherine had spent her two brief outings window-shopping. She saw at once that forty pounds would go nowhere; she would have to buy essentials during the first few weeks then save up. All the same, she was willing to wait until she had enough money to buy the kind of clothes she wanted; good clothes, well cut and well made.

On Saturday night she had gone to bed content; she had found her week's wages on the breakfast table, and that afternoon she had gone to Marks and Spencer and spent almost all of it on undies. A methodical girl, she had made a list of the clothes she intended to buy, and crossed out the first line with satisfaction; next week it would almost certainly have to be a dress, Marks and Spencer again, something simple and unobtrusive to tide her over until she could afford something better. And perhaps a nightie? She hated the plain cotton ones she had had for so long.

On Sunday the Graingers went to church. It was a major undertaking, getting them there, for they insisted on walking through the close, a journey which took a considerable time at their leisurely pace. Katherine, between them, her arms supporting them, was thankful that the sun shone and that the early morning frost had dwindled away. And when they reached the cathedral there was still quite a long walk through the vast building to the seats they always occupied. But once settled between them, she was able to flex her tired arms and look around her. It was some years since she had been there, and she looked around her with peaceful content. They were seated near the pulpit, and she had a splendid view of the great building; she would be able to come as often as she liked, she thought with satisfaction, for it was barely five minutes' walk for her. The opening hymn was announced, and she helped her companions to their feet as the choir processed to their stalls.

The congregation was a large one and leaving the cathedral took time. They were outside, beginning their slow progress back home, when Dr Fitzroy joined them. There was a young woman with him, tall and good-looking and beautifully dressed. Dodie, thought Katherine, bristling to instant dislike; and she was right, for the young woman bent to kiss the old lady and then pat her grandfather on his arm with a gentle pressure.

'Darlings!' she declared in a clear, high voice. 'How lovely to see you, and how well you look.'

She had very blue eyes; she turned them on Katherine for an indifferent moment. Her nod, when the doctor introduced Katherine, was perfunctory.

'So clever of you, Jason, to find someone so suitable.'

'I can't take any credit for that,' he said placidly. 'Katherine more or less dropped into my lap—an answer to prayer, shall we say.' He smiled at Katherine, who was vexed to feel her cheeks redden. 'You've settled in? No snags?'

'None, Dr Fitzroy.' She heard her voice, very stiff and wooden and awkward-sounding, but for the life of her she couldn't do anything about it.

Dodie gave a chuckle. 'I should think not indeed! These are the two dearest, sweetest people I know.' She kissed them both, smiled at Katherine quite brilliantly, and took the doctor's arm. 'We shall be late...'

His goodbyes were brief. Katherine, scooping her elderly companions on to each arm, heard Dodie's high, penetrating voice quite clearly as they walked away.

'She will do very well, Jason. Dreadfully dull, poor dear, but I dare say she's very grateful—living in a pleasant house, good food and wages...'

The doctor's reply, *if* he replied, was lost on the wind. Katherine subdued a violent wish to leave her two companions as from that moment and never see them or the doctor again. As for Dodie...words failed her. Common sense prevailed, of course; it was a good job and she *did* live pleasantly, and it was wonderful to have money to spend. She sighed soundlessly and turned her full attention to Mr Grainger, who was busy pulling the sermon to pieces. She would stay for ever, she mused, while she had the chance of seeing Dr Fitzroy. It was the height of stupidity to love someone who had no interest at all in you. Dodie had said that she was dull, she might as well be stupid, too!

CHAPTER THREE

OCTOBER had given way to November, and the late autumn sunshine had disappeared behind low banks of cloud, tearing around the sky, pushed to and fro by a ferocious wind. The Graingers didn't venture out; Katherine unpicked knitting, played bezique with Mr Grainger, read the newspapers to him and romantic novels to Mrs Grainger and, in between whiles, gave a hand around the house. The cleaning ladies who came each day were excellent workers, but they did their work and nothing more; Katherine, perceiving how Mrs Dowling's corns hurt, took to carrying the trays to and from the dining-room and, occasionally, when Mrs Dowling was in need of a rest, she dried the dishes and loaded and unloaded the dishwasher. Mrs Dowling always thanked her rather coldly for these small tasks, but her manner had softened considerably; the small, quiet girl was no threat to her authority, and she was proving a dab hand at keeping Mr and Mrs Grainger happy.

During the second week of Katherine's stay she was invited to go down to the kitchen each morning before she dressed and share Mrs Dowling's pot of tea, something she was happy to do, for it made a pleasant start to the day, sitting at the kitchen table, drinking Mrs Dowling's strong tea and listening to that lady's views on life in general and the household where she lived and worked in particular.

Within a very few days it was Katherine who carried the early morning tea trays up to Mr and Mrs Grainger. As she pointed out, she was going upstairs anyway, and it would save Mrs Dowling's corns. But although her days were filled by small chores she had two hours off each afternoon, something she looked forward to; there was so much to do and see. The cathedral was a never-ending source of interest; she pored over the Magna Carta in its library, studied the ancient manuscripts there, and wandered to and fro, examining the tombstones. When she had had her fill, she explored the narrow streets around the close, admiring the houses and wishing that she could live in one of them. The Graingers' house was delightful but, although she lived in it, she was aware that sooner or later they would die and she would be out of a job. She wondered who would have the house; probably Dodie, who certainly wouldn't want to employ her in any capacity.

Katherine paused to admire a particularly fine Georgian house bordering on to the close. Dodie wouldn't want her grandparents' house; she would be married to Dr Fitzroy by then, and he must surely have a house of his own. She had seen him when he visited his patients, of course, but she knew no more about him than the first time they had met.

At the end of her second week she took herself off to Marks and Spencer again, and bought a dress: pale grey with a white collar and a neat belt—unexciting, but she would not get tired of it as quickly as a brighter colour. She bore it back and wore it that evening. Examining herself in the long glass in her bedroom she was pleased with her appearance, for it was a distinct improvement on anything else hanging in her wardrobe.

She went downstairs feeling pleased with herself, and when Mrs Grainger observed, 'You look nice, Katherine,' she beamed with pleasure. A pity that Dr Fitzroy couldn't see her now...

The wish was father to the thought: she was setting Mrs Grainger's knitting to rights when Mrs Dowling opened the door. 'Dr Fitzroy,' she announced as he came into the room.

He had brought a book which Mr Grainger had wished to read, and stayed only briefly, but he paused by the door to ask Katherine, 'Everything is all right?' and when she said 'Yes,' he gave her a vague, kindly look. 'Splendid. You must be looking forward to buying yourself some pretty clothes. I'm sure if you ask her, Dodie will tell you where to go.'

Katherine's calm face gave away nothing of her feelings about this unfortunate remark. Nothing, just nothing would make her buy anything at a shop recommended by Dodie, even if she could afford it, which she couldn't. She said in a wooden voice, 'How kind,' and shot him a look of such rage that he blinked. There was more behind that composed face than he had thought, and he found himself interested to know what it was.

He said pleasantly, 'If you should want to visit

your brother, let me know. I could drive you out there.'

'That's very kind of you, but I hadn't planned to—to go back for a little while.' She could hardly tell him that her letters had gone unanswered and a visit from her would be unwelcome. Joyce had said that she didn't care if she never saw her again... 'I'm very happy here,' she told him, and wished him a polite goodnight. Before she undressed that evening, she took a good look at her image in the pier-glass in her room. There was nothing wrong with her new dress; it was suitable, cheap and completely lacking in high fashion, but then, high fashion was something quite useless for someone like herself. It was a very nice dress, she told herself defiantly, and next week she would buy some shoes; high-heeled and elegant. By Christmas she would have an adequate wardrobe; by the time she had bought the basic items, she would be able to save her money and start to pick and choose.

She got into bed, planning what she would buy; clothes which would make Dr Fitzroy look at her twice. She was just dropping off on her hopeful thought when Mr Grainger rang. He couldn't sleep, he complained, and would she get him a drink? Ovaltine or Bengers...

Another week went by, highlighted by the doctor's visits, always brief, during which he took blood pressures, listened carefully to his patients' mild complaints and went away again with barely a word to

Katherine. There was a visit from Dodie too, as brief as the doctor's had been. She arrived just as the old couple were preparing to take their afternoon nap, wrapped in a beautifully cut coat and wearing high patent-leather boots. She had been to the hairdressers, she explained and just had to pop in and see how her darlings were getting on, although she cut her grandfather short when he started to describe his bad chest, laughingly telling him to stop worrying.

'You'll live for ever, darling,' she told him and hugged him briefly. 'You know how it depresses me when you talk about being ill.' She perched on the arm of his chair. 'Let me tell you about the party I'm going to this evening...'

'Alone?' asked her grandmother.

'Of course not—Jason will take me. I've told him that he must. He's always at the hospital or seeing patients, such a bore...' She jumped up. 'I must go now—I've promised to meet someone...'

She went in a flurry of haste, leaving behind her a strong scent of Opium and an equally strong feeling in Katherine that she couldn't leave quickly enough.

It was difficult after that to get the Graingers to settle down to their naps, and there was only an hour left of Katherine's free time by the time they had finally dozed off. She got into her elderly raincoat, tied a scarf over her head, and hurried through the North Gate into the heart of the city.

She had a week's wages in her pocket, and this time it was to be a raincoat to replace the deplorable garment she was wearing. Marks and Spencer's was more than her pocket could afford; she plunged into Woolworth's.

There was a surprisingly good selection of clothing; she found what she wanted and put it on, a sensible garment in lovat, but it felt comfortable and fitted well. With the money she still had, she nipped along to a small hat shop on the further side of the High Street and invested in a green felt hat; it was plain with its small brim and plain ribbon, but it suited her and it went well with the raincoat.

She hurried back to the close, stuffed the old raincoat into the dustbin at the back of the house with glee, and went in through the kitchen door. Mrs Dowling was there, getting the tea tray ready. She glanced up and said severely, 'Been spending your money again...burns a hole in your pocket, doesn't it?'

'Well, no, not really.' Katherine went to the kitchen glass and took a satisfied look at the hat. 'You see, I haven't had any new clothes for two years, and I've almost nothing to wear. I don't want Mr and Mrs Grainger to feel ashamed of me.' She added fervently, 'I hope it rains on Sunday so that I can wear this.'

It was several days later, soon after the doctor's usual visit, that Mr Grainger complained of not feeling well. He had just eaten a splendid tea, after an equally special lunch of soup, cheese soufflé and one of Mrs Dowling's egg custards, and Katherine decided that he had probably overeaten. She fetched

his indigestion tablets, settled him for another nap
and, since Mrs Grainger was disinclined for sleep,
found one of the novels that lady delighted in, and
sat down to read to her. It was the one time in the
day that she should have called her own, but it was
raining anyway, and she had no plans of her own.
Mr Grainger snored on the other side of the hearth
and woke refreshed, so that they presently dispersed
to tidy themselves for the evening.

Mrs Dowling was a first-class cook; they sat down
to prawn cocktails, minute steaks with a variety of
vegetables and one of her delicious trifles. They
played three-handed whist afterwards, until Katherine shepherded them to their rooms and went to the
kitchen to get their hot drinks.

Mrs Grainger was already in bed, awaiting the rit-
ual of her drink and the arranging of the various
objects on her night table which were designed to
get her through the night hours. Katherine put everything just so and went along to say goodnight to
Mr Grainger. He was sitting up in bed, and she
thought uneasily that he looked a bad colour and was
puffing a bit.

'Do you feel all right?' she asked him.

'Of course I do.' He sounded so testy that she
didn't say any more, but wished him a goodnight and
went back to the kitchen to tidy away the cups
and saucers before going to bed herself, to lie and
dream about Dr Fitzroy. A useless occupation, but
one she seemed unable to avoid.

Thinking about it afterwards, she had no idea what

had awakened her, but the sense of urgency caused her to put on her dressing-gown and slippers and go soft-footed first to Mrs Grainger's room. That lady was asleep, swathed in shawls, snoring lightly, so Katherine turned her steps towards Mr Grainger's room next door. There was a dim night-light by his bed; he liked to have that and by its faint glimmer she could see that he was sitting up in bed, struggling to breathe.

Dr Fitzroy had told her that the old gentleman had congestive heart failure, a condition he had had for some years, but which had been kept more or less stable. Now, to her frightened eyes, it had erupted with a vengeance. Her first thought was to fly to the telephone and get help, but her good sense sent her to the bedside to reassure the old man and then to open the window so that the over-warm room could cool off.

'You're perfectly all right,' declared Katherine stoutly. 'I know you can't breathe properly, but you'll feel better presently. I'm going to telephone Dr Fitzroy...'

She padded downstairs to the phone and rang the number he had given her. She was answered at once by a brisk, 'Yes, Dr Fitzroy speaking.'

'Oh, it's you,' said Katherine thankfully. 'Please will you come? Mr Grainger isn't well. He can't breathe properly.'

His calm voice sounded almost placid. 'I'll be with you in ten minutes. Leave the front door unlocked. Go back to Mr Grainger and keep him happy until I get there. Oh, and open a window.'

'I have.'

She heard his grunt of approval as she put the receiver down, glancing at the clock as she did so. Half-past five.

She unbolted the door and flew back upstairs, to find Mr Grainger puffing and panting. If he had had the breath, he would have been snarling with rage, too; he had never been a man to take kindly to illness, and he had no intention of changing his attitude now. He glared at Katherine and began to struggle from his bed. He was old, but he was a big, heavily built man still; she was struggling to keep him quiet against his pillows when Dr Fitzroy came quietly into the room. He didn't speak, only disentangled Katherine and Mr Grainger, laid his patient gently back and set her back on her feet.

'Now, let's see what we can do,' he observed. He could have been making one of his routine calls at a more conventional hour, the only difference being that he was dressed in casual trousers and a thick sweater. He smiled at Katherine and bent over his patient. His vast, calm presence did much to reassure the old gentleman; Mr Grainger still puffed and panted, but his furious panic had been checked. The doctor examined him without haste and then opened his bag. 'You'll do,' he said cheerfully. 'I'm going to give you something to let you sleep, and you'll feel perfectly all right when you wake up.' He drew up an injection and pushed up Mr Grainger's pyjama sleeve, slid in the needle and observed, 'I dare say you had too heavy a meal—I shall talk to Katherine presently and tell her what you can and can't eat, and you'll oblige me by listening to her if she warns you. I'm going to stay here until you drop off—you are quite all right now, so don't worry, and when I'm gone, Katherine will be here.'

He glanced across the bed to where she was standing, wrapped in the same useful garment in which he had first seen her. Her hair hung down her back, and she was a little pale from fright. There was nothing about her to attract his notice, and yet he glanced at her a second time, and this time she looked up and met his eyes. Not a nonentity, he decided then, not with those beautiful grey eyes. He smiled at her. 'We'll have a talk before I go,' he told her.

Mr Grainger's breathing had slowed to a reassuring, gentle snore. After five minutes or so, they left him, and Katherine led the way downstairs. 'I expect you would like a cup of tea? I'm sure Mrs Dowling won't mind if I make one.'

He put his bag on the kitchen table and sat down beside it. 'Have one with me? Now, listen carefully, and I will explain what you may expect from Mr Grainger...'

She made the tea and listened. She would have listened all night if he had chosen to go on talking, but he gave her explicit instructions, drank his tea and explained in simple terms exactly what was the matter with Mr Grainger.

'He is elderly, his heart is tired, and from time to

time he overdoes things and nature takes over and stops him. Mrs Grainger worries about him, so skim over the details if you can.' He smiled at her. 'Go back to bed for an hour or so. You'll be busy enough in the morning. I'll call in about lunch time, but telephone me if you're worried. The hospital will know how to find me.'

She didn't know what prompted her to ask, 'Do you live near here, Dr Fitzroy?' but she wished she hadn't spoken, for his, 'Yes, I do,' was uttered in a voice in which coolness and indifference were nicely blended.

It was the indifference which did it; she had spent two years with Henry and Joyce, fighting their intentions to turn her into a willing doormat, but her new-found freedom had made her courageous, and she said haughtily, 'I have no wish to pry, I merely wish to know how long it would take you to get here in an emergency.'

He got up from the table and stood looking at her; it was surprising how she grew on one, he thought, despite the fact that as far as he could see she looked no more glamorous than on the occasion of their first meeting. That terrible dressing-gown, fit for a jumble sale!

He asked, 'Have you been paid?'

'Yes—each week. It's over three weeks…'

He went to the door. 'Oh, good—so you *will* be able to buy yourself some pretty clothes.' He had his hand on the door-handle. 'Don't bother to see me out, I'll shut the door behind me.'

She watched him go, loving him to distraction and seething with bad temper. She washed the mugs and emptied the teapot and calculated how many weeks it would take before she could buy some really decent clothes. Not that he would notice!

In this she was quite correct; he had remarked that she would want to buy some clothes because he guessed that she had been deprived of that pleasure for far too long, but he had meant to be kind. He dismissed her from his thoughts as he drove back to his house.

Katherine didn't go back to bed. It was already half-past six, in half an hour Mrs Dowling would be getting up, and Katherine suspected that Mr Grainger was going to keep her fully occupied during the day. She went to her room and showered and dressed, and went downstairs again just as Mrs Dowling entered the kitchen.

'Well, I never heard a sound,' declared that lady when Katherine explained about the night's events. 'You've had a busy time of it. Sit down for a minute and I'm going to make us a cup of tea.'

After that, there was very little rest for Katherine. Mr Grainger, peevish at having to remain in bed, was prepared to dislike and disagree with everyone, and his wife, convinced that he was dying, spent a good deal of time sitting listlessly in a chair, only brightening when Katherine coaxed her to have something to eat or found time to read aloud one of the romantic novels she loved. Even Dr Fitzroy had difficulty in convincing her that her husband was in no danger.

All in all, it was a trying day for everyone, and Katherine, for one, was heartily glad when, her two charges safely in their beds and asleep, she was able to get into her own bed. She wondered, as she closed her eyes, why Dodie hadn't called; another pair of hands would have been welcome, and she professed a deep affection for her grandparents. She was asleep before she could pursue the matter.

The next two days were almost as bad, and on the third morning Dr Fitzroy called, declared that his patient was perfectly fit to get up again, warned him to keep to a light diet for a few days, and took himself off again with no more than a few words to Katherine, and those were concerning Mr and Mrs Grainger.

She showed him to the door, since Mrs Dowling was busy in the kitchen, and he paused on the step, nodded briefly and crossed the pavement to his car. Very touchy, she decided, closing the door after him. Probably, he worked too hard.

Dodie came that very afternoon, just as Katherine had got Mr Grainger out of bed and into a rather splendid dressing-gown, and helped him downstairs to where his wife was waiting in the sitting-room. Dodie was wearing a scarlet coat and soft leather boots, and swinging a shoulder bag to match them. She was as pretty as a picture, and no wonder the doctor doted on her, thought Katherine, wishing her a polite good afternoon.

'Darlings!' exclaimed Dodie, and swooped upon them both with little cries and hugs. 'I would have come sooner, but I had the teeniest cold and I was so afraid of you getting it.' She pulled up a stool and sat down between them. 'I've come to tea, if you'll have me.' She looked over her shoulder at Katherine. 'You can go out for half an hour, only be back by four o'clock. I suppose Mrs Dowling will get the tea?'

'I'll tell her you are here as I go,' said Katherine. 'That is, if Mr and Mrs Grainger don't mind me going out for a while?'

She was told to go; they would be perfectly all right with their darling Dodie to look after them. The two old people hardly looked up as she slipped out of the room.

It was nice to be outside again, even for half an hour. She walked down High Street and into the shopping arcade, looking in its windows—her next pay would have to go on shoes or boots. Shoes, she decided; the boots she liked were too pricey, but she could get some good shoes... She walked back, happily mulling over her future purchases.

The Bentley was parked outside the house as she reached it. She went upstairs, took off her outdoor things, tidied her hair and went to the sitting-room. Dodie was still there, her hat and coat cast over a chair now, fussing over her grandparents while Dr Fitzroy sat watching her. She looked up as Katherine went in.

'Oh, there you are,' she exclaimed, faintly reproachful. 'I was beginning to think you had forgotten the time. Can we have tea, do you suppose?'

Katherine said, 'Oh, of course,' and went along to the kitchen, swallowing resentment. Perhaps she had been away for too long but, after all, Dodie *had* said half an hour, and she had been exactly twenty-five minutes...

Mrs Dowling was looking impatient. 'Why don't they want their tea?' she wanted to know. 'Miss Dodie told me to wait until you got back, but I can't think why. I always take in the tea, and she's surely able to pour out?'

Katherine thought she knew the answer to that, but she didn't say so. 'I dare say Miss Dodie thinks I take up the tea,' she said peaceably. 'Dr Fitzroy's there...'

She fetched another cup and saucer from the dresser and picked up the tray. 'Do you mind if I take it? Miss Dodie seems to expect it.'

Mrs Dowling nodded rather coldly. 'Better if you do, I suppose, just this once.'

Katherine arranged the tea tray carefully on the round table by the window, and Dodie said carelessly, 'All right, Katherine, you can go back to the kitchen. We'll ring if we want anything.'

She had gone, closing the door quietly behind her, before Dr Fitzroy said quietly, 'I thought Katherine had tea here?'

'Oh, does she?' Dodie sounded vague. 'Well, I dare say she'll be glad of a chat with Mrs Dowling,' she declared, and added, so softly that her grandparents couldn't hear her easily, 'She's been happy enough to do that for the last few days.' She smiled at the doctor. 'I've popped in each afternoon, you know.'

He looked a little surprised. 'Oh, have you? That was thoughtful of you, Dodie.'

She pouted prettily at him. 'Just because I don't go around with my hair scraped back and no make-up doesn't mean to say that I'm not just as capable as any other girl.' She poured the tea, and urged tiny sandwiches and cakes upon the old people, looking the very picture of sweet domesticity.

Presently, on their way out, they met Katherine coming from the kitchen and the doctor stopped. 'I'm glad that you've had a little time to yourself in the afternoons.' he observed. 'Dodie tells me that she's been standing in for you.'

The hall was rather dim, so he missed the fleeting look of astonishment on her face. 'Oh—yes. It—was nice to get out.'

Dodie tugged his arm. 'Darling, do come on, I've a dinner date.' She looked across at him and on to Katherine, and a little smile curled at the corners of her mouth. 'I'll be here at the same time tomorrow, Katherine.'

Katherine shut the door after them; if Dodie came the next day, she was prepared to eat her week's wages!

It was a safe bet, there was no sign of her; but Mrs Dowling rather surprisingly offered to keep an eye on her employers while Katherine had an hour to herself after lunch. The weather had become wintry; Katherine bought a warm and pretty dressing-

gown and cosy slippers. She didn't mind getting up
in the night to tend her charges, but it was chilly in
the small hours.

The shops were beginning to show signs of Christmas; she drooled over the pretty things on display,
at the same time determined not to spend any more
money until she had at least three weeks' wages, so
that she could buy an outfit for Christmas. A coat, it
would have to be cloth and plain, and a dress to go
under it. Besides, there were presents to buy for
Henry and Joyce and the children. They wouldn't
want to see her, but all the same she had made up
her mind to take her gifts and wish them a happy
Christmas. Who knew, they might be glad to see
her...

Because she was determined not to buy anything,
she took another direction on the following afternoon, past the Graingers' house, circling the close,
past the King's House and on towards the Bishop's
Palace. The houses here were larger, in a variety of
architectural styles, most of it centuries old. Despite
the cold wind, she dawdled along, studying them
with pleasure, pretending to herself that she had the
choice of living in one of them. She found her ideal
presently: red-tiled gables, lattice windows and a
stout oak door, heavily nailed. Probably a mass of
small rooms and narrow passages, a nightmare to
keep clean, but all the same a house to love and
dream over. There was no one about. She loitered in
front of it, trying to picture its interior, momentarily
lost to her surroundings, so that when Dr Fitzroy said

quietly from behind her, 'Spying out the land, Katherine?' she gave a squeak, and whirled round to face him.

'Exploring,' she said, and beamed up at him. 'I've never been as far as this, only seen it from a distance when I've been to the cathedral.'

'I should have thought that you found the shops more interesting.'

'Oh, I go there too, but I'm saving up, and that's easier to do if I keep away from them.'

He said carelessly, 'Oh, Christmas presents and so on. Will you go to your brother's?'

She nodded. 'I hope they'll be glad to see me—just for an hour or two, I expect...' She paused, aware that, although he was listening, it was with the air of a man who had other things to do but didn't wish to be unkind. She felt the colour rush into her cheeks. 'I must go—I've come too far. Goodbye, Doctor.'

She whisked away, going at a great rate, and he stood and watched her small figure until it had disappeared round a curve in the road before crossing to the house she had been admiring and letting himself in.

It was the following afternoon, on her return from a brisk walk, that she went into the drawing-room and discovered that the Graingers had a visitor.

He was sitting between them before the fire, and it was obvious that they were enjoying his company. He turned to look at Katherine as she paused in the doorway, and then stood up. 'Ah, the estimable Katherine,' he said genially, and she felt a prick of resentment at his use of her name. 'I've been hearing about you and your many kindnesses to my aunt and uncle.'

They shook hands, which gave her the chance to study him, without appearing to do so. He was not young, forty, she judged, perhaps older, with a round, jovial face, pale blue eyes and receding hair, neither grey nor fair. He smiled too much, decided Katherine at once, and his hands were warm and a little damp. She didn't care for him at all, but she had no reason to dislike him and he seemed anxious to be on good terms with her. She replied suitably to his rather banal remarks, and went away to fetch the tea; it was one of those days when Mrs Dowling's corns were playing her up.

'Still there, is he?' asked that lady as Katherine went into the kitchen. 'And likely to stay, as far as I can see.' And, at Katherine's enquiring look, 'He's Mrs Grainger's step-nephew, if you see what I mean—his mother was her step-sister. Lives in Cheltenham—a bachelor—no money to speak of, but likes to spend it whether he's got it or no.'

Katherine received these confidences in prudent silence. No doubt Mrs Dowling would be annoyed with herself for airing them, later on. She picked up the tray and murmured suitably before going back to the drawing-room.

Perhaps she had been a bit hasty in her first opinion of the visitor, she reflected as she collected the tea things and bore them back to the kitchen. Tom Fetter hadn't put a foot wrong during tea. Indeed, he had kept the Graingers amused and interested, and they obviously liked him. It hadn't surprised her when Mrs Grainger had invited him to stay. 'For this is quite a large house and we would love to have you—it would be silly to go to a hotel. Besides, you have so much to tell us.'

The old lady was quite animated, and as for Mr Grainger, Katherine had never seen him so good-natured. She excused herself presently and went away to prepare a room for their unexpected visitor.

She was grateful that he didn't disrupt the mild routine which governed the household. He made no demur when she suggested to the old couple that it was their usual bedtime, and in the morning he arrived punctually at the breakfast table and then took himself off for a walk while Katherine organised the day.

Dr Fitzroy paid his usual visit in the morning, listened good-naturedly to his patients' long-winded account of their guest, pronounced himself satisfied with their health and suggested that Katherine should go with him to his car parked outside to fetch some tablets.

'Well?' he asked, once they were free of the street door. 'What do you think of this nephew? Can you cope with a guest in the house? Mrs Dowling has enough to do...'

For all the world, thought Katherine, as though I sit about all day reading novels... 'Of course I can,' she said rather tartly. 'He's very considerate, and he's someone new for them to talk to. They like having him here.'

'But you don't. And don't frown at me like that, Katherine. Your face is like an open book when it comes to feelings.'

She went pink, and looked at him with such horror that he added, 'Now what have I said? You look as though I've caught you stealing...'

He might say that he could read her thoughts, but he hadn't discovered that she was head over heels in love with him; she thanked heaven fervently for that, managed a smile and decided not to answer him.

Dodie came that afternoon, professed herself delighted to meet a member of the family she had heard of but never seen, and stayed for tea. She and Tom Fetter got on splendidly, and when she got up to go he offered to walk with her.

In the hall, putting on her coat, Dodie asked, 'And how is our little paragon?' She glanced at Katherine and smiled brilliantly. 'Dr Fitzroy seems to think you are the eighth wonder of the world—I can't think why. Do you like him?'

Katherine said calmly, 'Yes, I do, he's been very kind to me and I'm happy here.'

'Just the kind of little willing work-horse he was looking for, and of course you think he is marvellous... You ought to see the nurses at the hospital falling over each other to work for him! He's got charm, all right, and knows how to use it, too. He comes home and tells me of some new conquest and we have a good laugh…' She got out a lipstick and studied her face in the hall mirror. 'Still, you're too sensible to get taken in, aren't you? I mean to say…he can take his pick of pretty girls, and I don't mind, he's not serious with them.' She smiled quite brilliantly again. 'I'm the one who matters.' She nodded. 'I thought I'd let you know that.'

Tom Fetter came into the hall, and she added, 'See you some time, Katherine,' and went away with him, leaving Katherine quite speechless. She had to stay where she was for a few minutes to calm down, for she found that she was shaking with rage. Why had Dodie told her that load of rubbish—for she was sure that that was what it was—unless, horrid thought, she had somehow guessed at Katherine's feelings for Dr Fitzroy? She went hot and cold at the very idea.

It surprised her when Dodie came the following afternoon and stayed to tea, and again Tom Fetter saw her home. The next day, he told Mrs Grainger that he was taking Dodie out to lunch.

'So nice that they are enjoying each other's company,' declared the old lady. 'He is such a splendid companion, isn't he, Katherine? So amusing and thoughtful. I'm sure we haven't enjoyed ourselves so much for a long time.'

And, true enough, he kept them happy, even though Katherine now found it difficult to keep them to the gentle routine Dr Fitzroy had mapped out for them. They wanted to stay up later, change their suitable diets for the more exotic dishes he was always describing to them.

At lunch, Mr Grainger said suddenly, 'I wish Tom lived with us, he's such splendid company. I did hint at it, but he says he has this very pleasant house in Cheltenham—too big for him, it seems, and costs a great deal to maintain...'

Katherine settled them for their afternoon nap, glad that the house was quiet, and then put on her outdoor things and went into the town. She had intended to save her week's wages, but she had seen, days ago, a winter coat in an unassuming peat-brown cloth, not quite what she had hoped to buy, but the days were becoming cold and a thick coat was a must. She hurried back with it, well pleased with her purchase, despite the fact that she had very little money left in her purse.

She went into the house through the kitchen door, and found Mrs Dowling loading the tea tray. 'I don't know why they're all here,' she complained, 'the doctor and Miss Dodie and that Mr Fetter, all wanting their tea.'

Katherine took off her outdoor things and laid the carrier bag containing the new coat carefully on top of them. 'I'll take the tea in,' she offered. 'They won't want me to stay, I'll come back here, if I may, and have tea with you.'

They all turned to look at her as she went in; the doctor took the tray from her as she murmured a good afternoon to the room in general and added, 'I'll just bring in the cakes and scones. I expect Miss Dodie will pour out.'

She whisked away and returned with a second

tray, which she laid on a side table before she made for the door once more.

'You'd better stay,' said the doctor. 'Mr Grainger has something to say to you.'

She turned slowly to face them all, all of a sudden aware that something awful was about to happen, a guess borne out by the sly look of satisfaction on Dodie's face.

CHAPTER FOUR

'LET me pour the tea first,' said Dodie gaily. 'And, Katherine, pass the scones round before you sit down.'

Katherine did as she had been asked. Dodie was making it worse, she guessed that, prolonging the moment when she was going to be told something which was going to shatter her newly found independence and contentment. She sat down presently, a cup and saucer in her hand, and took a sip of tea. She was going to need it before they had finished.

It surprised her a little that the doctor had said nothing, merely sat there, looking calmly from one to the other. Dodie went to sit beside him and laughed across at her grandfather. 'Now, darling, do tell Katherine what you've decided.'

She looked around the circle of faces, smiling prettily, quite sure that they were all enjoying themselves as much as she was. 'And I can't take all the credit for it,' she told them. 'Tom shared my idea and made it possible.'

'So, shall we hear what it is?' suggested the doctor. 'I, for one, can't spare more than a few more minutes.'

Old Mr Grainger coughed importantly and glanced across at his wife. 'Well, it's like this,' he began.

'Dodie, bless the darling child, thinks that a change of scene would do us good, and Tom here has invited us to go back with him to Cheltenham—and we've agreed...' He was interrupted by Mrs Dowling coming quietly into the room to whisper into the doctor's ear. He got up at once, excused himself and left the room with her, to return within a few moments. 'I have to go to the hospital—something has come up...' He glanced briefly at Katherine, and then at Mr Grainger. 'Perhaps we can talk about this later?'

He didn't stay for an answer.

A pity he had been called away, reflected Katherine, listening to plans being made—plans in which she was not included. 'We will give you a splendid reference,' Mr Grainger told her, 'and I'm sure you'll find another job at once, Katherine. Why, Dodie tells me that she knows of several people who would love to have you. We can't take you with us, you understand. Tom's house isn't large enough for that, and we plan to stay some months.'

He looked at his wife and went on, 'Mrs Dowling will stay on here, of course, and you are most welcome to remain until you move to another job.'

Katherine found her voice, and marvelled that it sounded just as usual. 'When do you intend to go?'

'Within a few days. There will be a few arrangements to make, and the packing, but, of course, you will be here to do that.'

She agreed calmly, and if her face was pale she didn't allow her dismay to show; she wasn't going to give Dodie the satisfaction of that. She wondered why

Dodie hadn't persuaded her grandparents to ask her to go with them—she would have been out of the way then, and that was obviously what she wanted. So silly, really: Dodie had never been in any danger of losing the doctor to her. Her vague speculations were cleared almost at once.

'I know just the job for you,' declared Dodie. 'A nice old couple who live near Stockbridge—rather rural, but then you like the country, I expect.'

'I'm sure I'll be able to find work, but it's kind of you to bother.' Katherine stood up. 'Shall I clear the tea things? I expect you have a lot to discuss. I'll be in the kitchen.'

She went unhurriedly from the room, her throat so choked by tears that, when she reached the kitchen, she couldn't speak. Mrs Dowling took one look at her, took the tray and asked, 'Bad news? I had a feeling it was. Sit down and I'll make a cup of tea, and you can tell me if you want to.'

Katherine wasn't going to cry, but she couldn't speak either, so she nodded her head and sat down at the table. The tea, a strong brew favoured by the housekeeper, steadied her. She was able to tell Mrs Dowling the plans which had been made, and ended, 'You don't have to worry, you're to stay here while they're gone.'

Mrs Dowling nodded. 'Suits me, but what about you? Turning you off at a moment's notice, I can't understand it! You've been such a help, and they like you.'

'But Mr Fetter amuses them...'

'Don't trust the man, myself,' declared Mrs Dowling.

Katherine was inclined to agree with her when, the following morning, coming downstairs after searching for Mrs Grainger's spectacles, she overheard Mr Grainger's voice, always rather loud. 'You're sure five thousand is enough, Tom? And of course we'll arrange for extra help in the house while we're with you. Just let me have the bills—you'll have a good deal of extra expense...'

It wasn't her business, of course, and Mr Fetter was a kind of relation. But there had been no need for him to invite the Graingers to his house; they had been happy enough. She hoped there would be someone at his home to fetch and carry for the elderly pair. She handed over the spectacles and began to unravel Mrs Grainger's knitting, wondering what Dr Fitzroy would have to say when he was told.

He came half an hour later, gave his brief examinations, asked to sit down for a few moments, then did so.

He heard Mr Grainger's news with no sign of disquiet, and that was something Katherine hadn't expected.

'I see that you are determined to go,' he observed calmly, 'and I imagine that there is nothing I can say which will make you change your mind? I cannot say that I like the idea, though. And whose idea was it?'

Mrs Grainger said excitedly, 'Dodie's, bless her, always thinking of us—and Tom was only too ready to fall in with her plans. She had them all settled for us, too. We shall go in a couple of days' time, Katherine will ʼack for us...'

'She goes with you?' He didn't look at Katherine as he spoke.

'Oh, no! Dodie says there is no need, Tom will have plenty of help at his home. We shall miss her, of course, but I'm sure she'll find more work easily enough.'

She glanced at Katherine and smiled. 'Dodie knows some people near Stockbridge...'

He said easily, 'I don't think you need to worry about Katherine.' He got up. 'I'll come the day after tomorrow and give you both a check-up and let a colleague of mine in Cheltenham know that you'll be staying there for a time. You're quite sure that you want to go?'

It was Mr Grainger who replied, 'Quite sure, Jason. Of course, you'll keep an eye on us when we get back?'

'Of course.' He bade them a pleasant goodbye, and Katherine went with him to see him out.

At the door he said briskly. 'I shouldn't worry about finding work. Something will turn up.'

She agreed quietly, watching him cross the pavement to his car. He hadn't even offered to give her a reference. A great wash of self-pity threatened to swamp her. If only she hadn't spent almost all her money on a coat! The week's wages she would be paid wouldn't go far. She fought back tears; being sorry for herself was no help at all. She gave a defiant sniff and went up to the attics to fetch the cases needed for packing.

She was kept fully occupied after that, packing and then unpacking again, because Mrs Grainger couldn't make up her mind what she wanted to take with her. Mr Fetter was much in evidence, laughing a great deal, making rather grandiose plans and, when Dodie called, which she did each day, falling in with her own plans to visit them in Cheltenham. It all sounded delightful, but Katherine didn't feel very happy about it. Somehow, Tom Fetter didn't sound quite right, although she didn't know why. Perhaps he laughed too much, and when he wasn't laughing he was smiling, and yet his eyes were restless, as though he expected someone to query his good humour. Not that it concerned her, she reminded herself sternly; on the following day they would all be gone and she would have started looking for work. Mr Grainger had given her an extra week's wages and told her that she might stay at the house until she found something else to do, so that her immediate worries had been quietened. All the same, on the last evening, after she had seen the Graingers safely into their beds, she had gone to her room and packed. Surely she would find work within the next day or two?

It was something of a chaotic morning. Mr and Mrs Grainger took time to prepare themselves for their trip, various comforts for the journey needed to be stowed about their persons, cases—already packed— had to be opened and checked, and a variety of instructions needed to be given to Mrs Dowling. At the last minute, Dr Fitzroy had driven up, got out of his car and strolled over to say a final goodbye. That done, he turned to Tom Fetter, who was fussing round his car.

'I've telephoned Dr Carver, a friend of mine in Cheltenham. He promises that he will attend Mr and Mrs Grainger. You do realise that they need medical supervision regularly?'

'My dear chap,' began Tom Fetter, 'I wasn't born yesterday—you medics aren't the only people with brains. I'll keep a sharp eye on them, never fear.'

Dr Fitzroy nodded. 'As you like—as long as you understand your responsibilities. Dr Carver will keep me informed.'

Tom Fetter laughed uneasily. 'Good lord, you sound as though you don't trust me.'

To this, the doctor made no reply, merely turned on his heel, got into his car and drove away. He had neither looked nor spoken to Katherine, and she watched him go with mixed feelings: bitter regret that she was unlikely to see him again, and a waspish desire to say something really nasty if ever she did. She was discovering it was hard to love someone who completely ignored her.

The house was very quiet once they had all gone; Dodie had been there to see them go, but she hadn't stayed. 'I expected Jason to be here,' she had grumbled. 'I told him to wait for me.' She had flounced off, looking cross.

It was nice to be kept busy for the next hour or two; there was really no need for Katherine to help

Mrs Dowling, for the daily cleaner was there and was to stay all day, but it kept her occupied—stripping beds and getting the rooms ready for what Mrs Dowling called a good turn-out. After lunch, Katherine went into the city and sought out the agencies she had looked up in the telephone directory. She visited three, and none of them had anything suitable; she couldn't type, and although she could cook she had no cordon bleu qualifications, nor had she any nursing experience. She was advised to return in a few days; home helps were always in demand, she was told encouragingly, but of course, with Christmas not far off, most people had made their arrangements well ahead. She went back to the house, not exactly worried, but vaguely apprehensive.

She spent the next day round the house, polishing the silver for Mrs Dowling and wrapping it carefully in baize so that it might be taken to the bank for safe-keeping. She was putting on the kettle for tea when Dodie arrived.

'Still here?' She sounded annoyed. 'I'll give you the address of those people at Stockbridge. You can get a bus there tomorrow and be interviewed. They're desperate for someone, so there's no doubt that you'll get the job.'

Katherine thanked her with a calm she didn't feel. Dodie had been the means of her losing her job with the Graingers, and now she was trying to push her into a household she knew nothing about, and buried in the country to boot! She had no intention of going there, but there was no point in annoying Dodie. That young lady departed presently, well pleased with herself, having left exact instructions as to how Katherine was to get to the place. 'I'll phone this evening and let them know you're coming,' she promised.

Mrs Dowling was going to spend the night with her sister who lived on the other side of Salisbury; it was a chance, she explained to Katherine, which she might not get again for a long time, for, once Katherine had gone, she didn't feel she could leave the house empty. 'You don't mind?' she wanted to know. 'You're not nervous?'

'Not a bit,' declared Katherine, and promised to shoot every bolt, double lock the doors and close every window before she went to bed.

All the same, the old house seemed very empty, even with the TV on. She went to bed early, her head full of plans for getting a job as quickly as possible in Salisbury, plans hindered by thoughts which had nothing to do with them and wholly to do with Dr Fitzroy.

She got up early in the dark of the winter morning, made herself tea and set about getting breakfast. Mrs Dowling would be back for lunch, and she would have ample time to go back to the agencies and try her luck once again. She was making toast when the bell rang.

The postman, probably, with Christmas parcels—a bit early, but some people always posted them too soon… She undid the bolts, turned the key in the lock and took down the chain. She found the doctor on the doorstep.

'My goodness, you are up early!' said Katherine. 'Is something wrong?' She ushered him inside, full of delight at the sight of him. 'I've just made breakfast. Would you like a cup of tea?'

'Please. I've been at the hospital since four o'clock. I wanted to see you, and this seemed a good opportunity.'

He followed her through the house, and she sat him down at the kitchen table, poured tea and put a plate and the toast before him. He looked tired and hungry, and she offered him eggs and bacon.

'Oh, splendid, but only if you're cooking for yourself. Where's Mrs Dowling?'

'She's spending the night with her sister. She'll be back by midday.'

'You've been alone in the house?'

Her delight at seeing him again was fading in the remembered disappointment at his lack of interest in her future. Perhaps he thought that, since he had given her a chance to get away from her brother, that was sufficient; and, in all fairness, probably it was.

All the same, she gave him a resentful look, and said with something of a snap, 'Well, of course.'

He was sitting at the table still, finishing off the toast. He said slowly, 'You're angry, aren't you? Left out on a limb—no job, no home, no future. Don't bother to deny it,' he finished blandly, 'I can see it for myself. You've been looking for work?'

She broke eggs with considerable force. 'Yes.'

'Well, don't. There is a job waiting for you at the

hospital.' He took another bite of toast. 'They're desperate for nursing aides—you know what they are?'

'Vaguely.' She ignored the sudden leap of hope; she hadn't got the job yet, she might be quite unsuitable. Besides, she didn't know much about nursing.

'Monotonous work, mostly: getting beds made, fetching and carrying for the nurses, feeding patients, carrying bedpans, cleaning up when someone's sick, but, if you're good at these, in time you will get more skilled work. The pay seems quite good...' He mentioned a sum which was a good deal more than the Graingers had been paying her. 'You get cheap meals in the canteen and, if you want to live out, my housekeeper has a sister who lets lodgings.' He sat back in his chair. 'Has it struck you that we tend to meet in the early mornings? Hardly romantic...'

'I don't think I'm a romantic person,' observed Katherine, piling bacon on to a plate and topping it with eggs. 'And you don't need to be...'

'What do you mean?'

'Well, there's Dodie...I mean, well...' She paused, trying to find the right words. 'You've found someone to be romantic about, so you don't need to bother any more.'

He gave a great snort of laughter. 'Remind me some time to put you right about one or two things! I must say you have some strange notions.'

He began his breakfast as she sat down with her own plate. 'Well, what about this job at the hospital? Do you want it?'

She poured him more tea, and said soberly, 'Yes, please. That is, if I'll do.'

'Good, I'll let you have the particulars some time today.'

'Thank you for bothering, Dr Fitzroy.' She was brimming over with relief and excitement, but she spoke with her usual calm.

'Did you think that I'd washed my hands of you? No, don't answer that.' He finished his breakfast and sighed. 'Will you forgive me if I go? I'm due to start work very shortly.'

He got to his feet, and she followed him out of the kitchen. 'Mr and Mrs Grainger—they'll be all right? I'd got rather fond of them. As long as there is some-one to look after them...'

'I shall make it my business to check on that. They were fond of you, too. They should never have gone on this visit, but Dodie persuaded them—and this Tom Fetter backed her up.'

She would have liked to have talked about that, but she could see that he wanted to leave. She opened the door and wished him goodbye. She stood at the open door, watching him drive away, thinking it would be wonderful to work near him and see him each day.

There was a phone call from the people at Stockbridge later that morning; a voice wanting to know when she would come. It seemed the owner of the voice was desperate—four children, home for the Christmas holidays, and an old granny to look after. Katherine explained with polite firmness that she already had a job, listened patiently to the moaning voice at the other end of the line and rang off. A fine thing, she told herself, if the hospital decided that they didn't want her, after all!

But it seemed that they did; Christmas holidays, 'flu and a sudden influx of patients had made it an urgent matter to enrol more help as quickly as possible. The rather severe voice asked her to go for an interview that afternoon and, if suitable, to be ready to start work a day or so later. It was usual, the voice went on, for several days to elapse while references were checked, but Dr Fitzroy had vouched for her.

Katherine reviewed her wardrobe, assembled a light lunch for herself and Mrs Dowling, and spent some time before the dressing-table glass, making the best of her appearance. After a meal with that lady, she put on the brown coat and walked to the hospital.

She had no idea what to expect. She presented herself at the reception desk, and was led by a rather harassed clerk to the back of the hospital, an area of gloomy corridors and massive doors, relieved only by the busts of former consultants, each on his or her plinth. By the time they reached their destination she was beginning to regret ever having come; the place overawed her, and even the atmosphere—composed of a chilly dampness, old age and a faint hint of Jeyes fluid—was off-putting.

But she had no time to change her mind; the clerk tapped on a door, opened it and ushered her briskly inside.

The room was small, dark, and overcrowded by a vast desk bearing a large quantity of papers, two telephones and a tabby cat. Behind the desk sat the lady she had come to see—formidable in appearance, with a vast bosom straining against her severe dress and severe hairstyle, but she had a kind face and she was smiling. Katherine took heart and advanced a step or two.

'Sit down, Miss Marsh. Dr Fitzroy has told me all about you, and I think that the best thing is for you to come here and work for a month and see if you like the job. I must warn you that it's hard work; we're short of staff and you may find the routine boring. Your salary...' She refreshed her memory from the papers before her, then mentioned a sum which seemed magnificent to Katherine. 'Of course, we don't usually take girls like this, but Dr Fitzroy recommends you highly, and we really are desperate.' She bent forward to stroke the cat. 'Do you need time to think it over?'

'No, thank you. I do need work badly, and Dr Fitzroy seemed to think that I might do. I'll come when you want me to.'

'Good. There will be forms to fill in and so on. Perhaps you could do that on your way out—reception will tell you where to go, and shall we say the day after tomorrow? I will let you know where to report for duty and at what time. You do understand that nothing is binding for the first month? You can leave with a week's notice on either side.' She nodded majestically and Katherine got up, put her chair tidily back against the wall and made her way back to the reception desk. Her head full of directions, she went

off again to find the office where she was to fill in
the forms; she got lost once or twice, and it was considerably later by the time she was ready to leave.
She was making her way rather uncertainly along a
narrow passage when she ran full tilt into Dr Fitzroy.

He put out a hand to steady her, remarking, 'Ah,
there you are. Everything settled?'

'Yes, thank you. I've just filled in lots of forms...'

He said kindly, 'Splendid! I asked my housekeeper
if her sister had any rooms to let. She has; if you'd
like to call round there she will fix you up—unless
you want to live in the hospital?'

'Oh, I'd love a room of my own.'

'Yes, well, here's the address.' He fished out a pen
and a notebook and scribbled in it, tore out the page
and gave it to her. 'Say that I sent you. Let me know
if you need any help.'

He nodded, and she could see that he was already
thinking about something else. She murmured,
'Thank you,' and moved away to be stopped by his,
'How are you off for money? Did the Graingers pay
you? Have you enough to see you through until pay
day?'

'Yes, thank you.'

His 'Good, good,' was uttered in an absent-minded
fashion, and his smile was vague, even though kind.
She watched him stride off, vowing to herself that
never, never would she ask him for help. He had been
kind, and offered practical help when she needed it,
but she wasn't going to make a nuisance of herself.
She watched lovingly until he had gone, and then

took herself out of the hospital and into the streets, intent on finding the address he had given her.

It was a small, neat house, in a row of similar dwellings quite close to the cathedral, although the narrow little street was quiet. She knocked on the door and a cosy, middle-aged woman opened it. Before Katherine could speak, she said, 'You'll be the young lady Dr Fitzroy told me about. Come in out from the cold and I'll show you the room.'

She led the way upstairs, talking over her shoulder as she went. On the landing, she said apologetically, 'It's on the top floor—used to be an attic, but I had it done up a bit, and there's a lovely view...'

It was quite large, with a sloping ceiling and a dormer window overlooking the nearby close. The furniture was simple but comfortable, and the floor was carpeted. There was a washbasin in one corner and a small gas fire, and in the opposite corner an old-fashioned gas cooker with two rings and a grill, and above it shelves neatly stacked with china and a few pots and pans.

'You can have a hot meal downstairs, but get your own breakfast here. Bathroom's downstairs and there's always plenty of hot water.'

She studied Katherine's face. 'Going to work at the hospital, are you, miss? Nursing aide? You'll not be earning all that much, then?' She named the rent and added, 'That'll include a good hot meal, baths and the use of the washing machine once a week. There's an iron when you need it, just as long as you ask first.

There's only three others here—two elderly ladies, and a lady clerk from the post office.'

'Oh, I'll take it, Mrs...?'

'Mrs Potts. Mr Potts passed on two years ago.'

'I think it's very nice here, Mrs Potts, and I'd like to rent the room. Do you want a month's rent now?'

'A week only, and a week's notice on either side. When do you want to come?'

'Tomorrow? In the afternoon?' As they went back downstairs, she said, 'I'm not sure, but I believe I have to do night duty from time to time.'

'I'll give you a key, and you can come and go as you please.' Mrs Potts eyed her severely. 'I only let to the decent sort of person I can trust with the door key.'

Katherine handed over a week's rent, and took herself back to the Graingers' house to take a substantial tea with Mrs Dowling and speculate over her future.

The next day, she bade Mrs Dowling goodbye with some regret; they had become not exactly friends, but at least they respected each other, and Mrs Dowling had been grudgingly grateful for the running to and fro Katherine had done for her. Bidden to have tea with the housekeeper when she was free, Katherine agreed; she had made no friends since she had been in Salisbury, but until now she hadn't had much time for that. Now she felt rather lonely. But not for long, she told herself bracingly, there would be other girls like herself working in the hospital.

It wasn't far to Mrs Potts', but her cases were heavy; she was glad to put them down on the doorstep and ring the bell. Mrs Potts opened the door, helped her upstairs with the cases, told her that there was tea in the pot downstairs, pointed out that a fifty-pence piece would provide her with warmth from the gas fire, and left her to look around her new home.

There had been a letter from the hospital that morning, telling her to report for work at eight o'clock in the morning. She was to go first to the office, where someone would take her to collect her uniform and show her the ward she was to work on. She had gone straight out and bought a cheap alarm clock, and carefully calculated how long it would take her to walk to the hospital. There was a back way through a car park which would save a lot of time. She had bought tea and a loaf and butter, too, and perhaps Mrs Potts could get the milkman to leave her some milk... She tapped on the kitchen door and went in.

Mrs Potts sat her down at the table, poured her a cup of tea and pressed a plate of scones upon her. 'There's supper at eight o'clock,' she explained. 'We have it here. I've put a jug of milk on the side for you. You've got some groceries?'

Katherine said thank you, she had, but she would be glad if she could have milk delivered, and added, 'I have to be at the hospital at eight o'clock tomorrow morning. They didn't say how long I would be working.'

'If you're not back by supper time, which I doubt, I'll keep something hot for you. Now, you go and unpack, and come down sharp at eight o'clock. We sit down punctually.'

Katherine unpacked, set her brushes and comb and modest make-up on the dressing-table under the window, hung her scanty wardrobe in the cupboard at one end of the room, arranged the photos of her parents on the narrow little mantelshelf, and sat down on the bed to survey her surroundings.

With the gas fire lit, it looked quite cosy, and on pay day she promised herself she would go to Woolworth's and buy a pretty table lamp. She had been lucky, she reflected; she had a job, a room of her own and more money than she had had for some years. Life wasn't going to be quite as comfortable as it had been with the Graingers, but a great deal better than it had been with her brother...

At eight o'clock she went downstairs, where she met her fellow lodgers. The elderly ladies greeted her politely; Miss Fish and Mrs Dunster, they looked rather alike—faded, genteel and faintly suspicious of her. Miss Kendall, on the other hand, shook hands firmly, declared that it would be pleasant to have someone of her own age in the house, and begged Katherine to call her Shirley. She was a big girl, excessively jolly, who had very little to say to her fellow lodgers, just as it was obvious to Katherine that they had very little to say to her. It was Mrs Potts who, as it were, leavened the dough, keeping up a cheerful conversation first with one side and then the other, so that, even though they didn't actually address each other, they appeared to do so. Katherine was seized upon almost at once as a kind of go-between, with the two elderly ladies plying her with guarded questions as to her family and her work, and Shirley drowning their mild remarks with questions of her own, while Mrs Potts filled in the pauses with some prosaic remark about the weather.

The food was excellent; Mrs Potts was a super cook, and her steak and kidney pudding, followed by apple tart and custard, bore witness to that. Katherine hadn't realised that she was so hungry, and sat back with a satisfied sigh as Mrs Potts put the teapot on the table and handed round cups of strong tea. She had just finished hers when Mrs Potts went to answer the doorbell, and came back almost at once.

'For you, Miss Marsh. Dr Fitzroy—I've put him in the front room.'

A forbidding apartment, seldom used except for interviewing lodgers, sitting in on Sunday afternoons and entertaining guests. Katherine went down the narrow hall and opened the door. The doctor was standing before the curtained window, looking very large and excessively tall. He turned round as she went in and his 'Hello, Katherine' was friendly. 'Having suggested that you should come here, I felt it my duty to come and see if you are comfortable,' he explained, and gave her a kindly smile.

She stood just inside the door, her heart beating a great deal too fast, trying to keep her breathing at a normal rate. He might have come from a sense of obligation, but at least he had come. She beamed at him widely.

'That's awfully kind of you, Dr Fitzroy. I'm very

happy with everything here. I've a lovely room, and Mrs Potts is so kind and the food is super.'

'Good. You know where you have to go tomorrow?'

'I had a letter from the hospital. I'm—I'm very grateful to you for all you've done. You have no idea how marvellous it is to have a job and so much money, and also somewhere to live...' She added in her quiet voice, 'I'll work hard, I promise you, and not let you down.'

He stared down at her, not smiling. 'I don't imagine you have ever done that, Katherine—let anyone down. I'm glad to hear that you are settled in here; if you need anything or you want help at any time, please come to let me know.' He sighed. 'You deserve better than this.'

She gave him an astonished look. 'But I'm not trained for anything, and if it hadn't been for you I wouldn't have this job. Please don't worry about me; I shall do very well, and I really am happy.'

Well, not happy, she told herself silently; how could one be happy when one loved a man and knew that he would never feel the least urge to love one in return? Their paths through life were widely separated, and she must never forget that.

He made a small gesture, and she felt that he was impatient to be gone. 'It was kind of you to call,' she said briskly, 'and if I need help I'll let you know, but I'm quite sure I'll be all right.'

She held out her hand, and he shook it and went on holding it. 'You're rather small,' he observed.

'But tough.' She pulled her hand gently to free it, and found it clasped more tightly...

When he bent and gently kissed her cheek, she held her breath. Before she could think of anything to say he had gone, his goodbye echoing from the closing door.

She went back to the kitchen presently and drank her cooling tea, helped to clear the table and then went up to her room. He hadn't meant anything by the kiss, she knew that, but it had unsettled her. She undressed, went down to the landing below, had a bath and then climbed into bed. She had a lot to think about, but she went to sleep at once, her head full of Dr Fitzroy.

CHAPTER FIVE

THE hospital, when Katherine reached it the next morning, was a subdued hive of activity. She was whisked from reception to the office, handed over to a stern-featured lady in a white overall, and fitted out with her uniform: biscuit-coloured stripes, an armful of aprons and several thick paper caps. She was told to change and, while she did so, the stern lady made up a cap for her. The uniform didn't fit very well, there seemed to be a good deal of extra material everywhere. Katherine gathered it into the striped belt and pinned a cap on her head. Her mentor shook her head in a despairing way, and led her up and down a vast number of corridors before pushing open swing doors. 'You're to work here,' she said, and went away.

The doors led to a wide corridor with more swing doors at its end and doors on either side. There wasn't much point in standing there doing nothing, Katherine decided, so she advanced along the corridor, peering in the half open doors as she went. Which brought her to Sister's office.

She knocked on the door and went in, and the woman at the desk looked up. She had severe features, scraped-back hair and eyes like dark pebbles, and Katherine knew at once that Sister wasn't pleased to see her. All the same, she said politely, 'I was told to come here to work, Sister. Katherine Marsh.'

Sister put down her pen. 'The girl Dr Fitzroy recruited. Why I should have you, I don't know; probably he didn't want to find you under his feet in his own wards. Have you done any nursing?'

'No, Sister. Just looking after Mr and Mrs Grainger, an elderly couple, and before that I looked after children.'

'Well, at least you're a pair of hands. You don't look very strong.'

Katherine didn't answer that, but waited for Sister to speak again. 'You're quite untrained, Staff Nurse will show you how best you can help in the ward. You are here on a week's trial, Miss Marsh. It's up to you to do your best.'

She bent her head over her desk, and Katherine got herself into the corridor again. Find Staff Nurse? Walk on to the ward? Tear off her apron and run like mad? Her problem was solved for her. A girl, dressed in a similar uniform to her, came bouncing out of one of the doors. She stopped when she saw Katherine.

'You're the new auxiliary,' she cried joyfully. 'Am I glad to see you! What's your name?'

'Katherine. I don't know where to go…'

The girl put out an arm and towed her along at a great rate to the doors at the end of the corridor. 'Miranda—everyone calls me Andy.' She beamed widely, and Katherine smiled back. Her companion was a big girl, with a mop of hair upon which her cap perched precariously, and a round, cheerful face. 'You don't need to know about nursing, not to start with, but it helps if you can do two things at once, carry trays, and clear out the sluice room!'

They were through the doors by then, to fetch up beside a small, fairylike creature in a blue dress with a red belt and a silver buckle. She was talking to a nurse, but she paused to say to Andy, 'Mr Sims hasn't had his paper again…' She cast her eyes over Katherine and went on, 'Ah, the new auxiliary. Good. Have you seen Sister?'

She smiled at Katherine in a friendly way, and Katherine, still feeling that she would like to turn and run for it, smiled back.

'Yes, Staff Nurse, she said that you would show me where to work.'

'Never nursed before? Not squeamish? Will you go with Andy and help with the bottle round? Then strip beds with her. When I've got five minutes, I'll give you an idea of the routine. In the meantime, just cling to Andy.'

Katherine had no idea of what a bottle round was; Andy explained rapidly as they went down the ward to the sluice room. It was a large ward, its beds filled, and its occupants, those who felt well enough, called out cheerfully as they went.

Andy threw replies to them in passing, and in the sluice said, 'They like to pass the time of day, but be careful when Sister's on the ward, she's man's natural enemy.' Andy handed Katherine something that looked like a milk bottle container. 'Got a boyfriend?'

'No, I don't know anybody in Salisbury.'

'Dr Fitzroy knows you, doesn't he? Weren't you looking after some private patients of his? He's a dream, isn't he? On the medical side, of course, so we hardly ever see him over here.'

Which perhaps, reflected Katherine soberly, was just as well. The morning was a cataclysm of half-understood work: she made beds, not very well, getting in a fearful muddle with the corners, urged on by the kindly Andy; she helped with the mid-morning drinks, scuttled up and down the ward fetching and carrying various odds and ends for any number of people, had to heave patients out of bed and in again, and always with Andy near at hand to urge her on or breathe encouragement. By lunch time she was tired, but by no means downhearted; if everyone else there could keep on their feet and know what they were about, then so could she. Not that she *was* always sure what she was about!

She was sent to first dinner with Andy, and told by Sister that she was to go off duty at five o'clock. 'You will work for a week with Miss Snell,' said Sister, indicating Andy, 'and after that you will work alternate duties with her. Come to the office when you report off duty, and I will tell you your duties for the week.'

'Do we always work like this?' asked Katherine, trotting along beside Andy on their way to the canteen. 'I mean, on the go the whole time?'

Andy laughed. 'This is a quiet week—next week's take-in. You should just see us then.' She was still explaining take-in when they reached the canteen.

'Take a tray—it's boiled beef and dumplings—I know one of the cooks. Have you got some money?'

Katherine nodded and watched her plate being piled high. Very good value for money, she reflected when she received it.

'Don't bother with a pudding,' advised Andy. 'Get a cup of tea.'

They found places at a table which was already well filled. Katherine was introduced to the half-dozen girls already there, and smiled a little shyly at them. They were a friendly bunch, full of helpful advice and hospital gossip as they gobbled their meal. 'A pity that you're with that old tyrant,' commented one of them. 'Sister Beecham is a tartar—talk about throwing you in at the deep end...'

There wasn't time to answer all their questions, much less ask any of her own; she found herself setting off again at Andy's heels, back to the ward. Afterwards, Sister went to second dinner and the ward wore a relaxed air in consequence.

Staff Nurse, busy with the medicine round, nodded cheerfully as they reported back on duty. 'There's some tea in the pot if you want a cup,' she told them. 'Only look sharp about it. Andy, take Mr Crouch down to X-ray as soon as you've had it; take Katherine with you so that she'll know where to go, and then make up the two end beds.' She turned back to her trolley and the student nurse with her, and Andy and Katherine hurried out to the kitchen where the teapot stood warming on the stove.

'We don't do this when Sister's on duty,' explained Andy quite unnecessarily.

X-ray was miles away, or so it seemed to Katherine, whose feet were aching madly, but once there she found it quite interesting. The patient was to have an operation for a duodenal ulcer, and needed a barium meal to confirm the surgeon's diagnosis. He was a cross old man, who contradicted everyone and found fault with each of them in turn. Half-way through the examination, Andy was sent for, leaving Katherine to stay with him. Presently, when the business was over, she was told to escort the trolley and porters back to the ward.

They were in the long corridor leading to the lifts when she saw Dr Fitzroy, accompanied by two young doctors in white coats, coming towards her.

He looked different—older and serious, very elegant in his dark, beautifully cut suit, his head slightly bent as he listened to his two companions' earnest talk. But he looked up as Katherine's little procession reached them, and gave her a brief, friendly smile. She wanted to smile too, but she thought she had better not. One of the nurses at dinner had been talking about him—he was important, a senior consultant, and he would be a professor in no time at all. 'And some lucky girl will get him,' the nurse had observed with ill-concealed envy. Katherine hadn't heard the rest of it. Crammed in the lift with the trolley, the patient and the porters, she reflected that the lucky girl was to be Dodie.

Five o'clock came at last, and with feet like hot

coals she went to Sister's office. Staff Nurse was there too, and gave her a friendly little nod, but Sister merely looked up, studied Katherine for a moment and said, 'You seem to be a good worker—time will show, however. Now, Miss Marsh, you're off duty…'

They were already near the end of the week, so she wouldn't get any days off until the following week—Thursday and Friday. In the meantime, she would have the same working hours as Andy: two days from noon until eight o'clock, two eight in the morning until five o'clock in the afternoon and, on the day before her days off, from eight o'clock until four in the afternoon. She would be paid on Thursday morning of the following week, and if she wished she could go to the office to collect her wages between the hours of ten and twelve o'clock.

She would get up early, thought Katherine happily, collect all that money and do her household shopping, join the local library, do some window shopping…

'I hope you are attending, Miss Marsh? It may be necessary from time to time to change your duty times. You must be prepared for that.'

Katherine said, 'Yes, Sister,' in her gentle voice, and smiled because she was, for the moment, happy. Sister very nearly smiled back. She stopped herself just in time; really, the girl wasn't at all the usual type—she hoped she would settle down and learn to do her work well.

'You may go, Miss Marsh,' she said austerely.

Katherine let herself in with the key Mrs Potts had given her, and went up to her room, kicked off her shoes, lit the gas fire and, resisting a strong desire to get into bed and sleep for ever, undressed and went down to the bathroom. The water was hot and plentiful; she lay in it blissfully, making mental lists of all the things she would buy. Only the cooling water got her out finally.

At supper, Mrs Potts wanted to know how she had got on.

'I enjoyed it,' said Katherine, and meant it. 'My feet ached, but I'll get used to that in a day or two.' She didn't say more than that, because Miss Fish and Mrs Dunster chorused a genteel objection to the discussion of one's work at the supper table. Shirley Kendall gave a loud laugh at that, and remarked rudely that honest workers had a right to do what they liked in their free time, and if they wanted to talk about their day's work, they should do so. 'At least some of us earn an honest living,' she remarked loudly.

The elderly ladies bridled at that, and Mrs Potts firmly put a stop to what might have been turned into an argument by offering second helpings.

Katherine went back to her room when the meal was finished, eased her feet into slippers and drew the elderly easy chair close to the fire. Half an hour's reading of the newspaper one of the patients had offered her would be very pleasant before bedtime. She yawned widely, and remembered with pleasure that she wasn't on duty until noon the next day. She would go to the shops and add to her small stock of groceries and have a look at the table lamps—not to buy of course, that would have to be the following week. She made another list, this time of things she needed to make her room a home, but she didn't quite finish it because she allowed her thoughts to wander. Where, she wondered wistfully, did Dr Fitzroy live, and in what kind of house? One day, when she knew Mrs Potts better, she would ask. On second thoughts, she decided against this; it was intruding into his private life.

She was up early, tidied her room, ate her frugal breakfast and took herself to the shops. Her few household needs were quickly dealt with; it would have been nice to have had a cup of coffee but, with an eye on her almost empty purse and two days off to allow for, she contented herself with window shopping.

She was peering into Jaeger's shop window, taking in all the stylish details of their winter coats and wondering if she would ever possess one, when she became aware of someone beside her. Dodie, looking as usual like a model in one of the glossier magazines. She also looked extremely cross.

She wasted no words in greeting. 'You ungrateful girl!' she said in an angry whisper. 'The trouble I took to phone those people at Stockbridge, and you didn't even bother to go for an interview.'

'Well, I didn't need to,' Katherine pointed out reasonably. 'I've got a job here. And I did tell you not to bother.'

'What sort of a job? Here? In Salisbury?'

It seemed that Katherine might be wiser not to say. She said calmly, 'Yes, here—looking after people.'

'All you're fit for,' observed Dodie unforgivably.

'Probably that's true,' agreed Katherine equably. 'Have you heard from Mr and Mrs Grainger?'

'Oh, they're all right. They won't stay with Tom, of course.' Her lovely blue eyes narrowed. 'But don't imagine that you'll get back your job with them, I've already arranged for a woman to be their companion when they return.'

'Why did you want me to go?' asked Katherine. She sounded politely interested, although her heart was thumping with rage.

'Jason—Dr Fitzroy was a fool to employ you in the first place—acted on the spur of the moment, out of pity, I suppose. He was only too glad when I fixed things so that you had to leave; saved him the embarrassment of getting rid of you.' She laughed nastily. 'I can't think why I'm bothering to tell you this.'

'Well, you're enjoying it, aren't you?' Katherine turned on her heel and dived into Country Casuals next door; there was a door at the other end of the shop which brought her into a shopping arcade where she could lose herself in the crowds. She didn't believe Dodie's spiteful remarks, but they had left a tiny doubt in her mind, none the less. Dr Fitzroy had made no effort to object when the Graingers had broached their plans, although he *had* found her another job. She looked at a few more shops, but her pleasure had gone; besides, it was time for her to go back to her attic with her shopping.

Whatever he had thought, she consoled herself, he had helped her to get a job and somewhere to live.

The days passed quickly. She had got the hang of the work within the week and, although she found it hard, she enjoyed it. Her feet ached and she was too tired to do much by the time she went off duty, but that was something Andy assured her would improve with time. Her keenly anticipated days off came at last, and with them pay day. She spent a lovely morning choosing a pretty lamp, having coffee and planning her days. She was still rather short of money. She had paid Mrs Potts the rent and laid out a carefully calculated sum on food, a hot-water bottle and dull things like tights; the rest she was going to save for an eiderdown for her bed and a thick sweater and skirt. She had seen exactly what she wanted. She bore the lamp back, made the tea, and opened a tin of beans and had her lunch by the gas fire.

It was a cold day but dry; she put on the new coat presently and went out again. A good walk would be very pleasant, right round the close perhaps, and then back for tea, and tomorrow she would go to the cathedral again and explore the Chapter House thoroughly.

Her way took her past the Graingers' house and along the narrow street towards the King's House.

Dr Fitzroy, standing at the window of his drawing-room, staring into the street, saw her, head down against the wind, her small, lonely figure the only thing moving there. He went to his front door and stood in the porch, and when she was near enough crossed the street.

Katherine stopped short as he fetched up in front of her. She didn't speak, only stared up at him in surprise. He said kindly, 'Hello, Katherine. Enjoying days off?'

A little colour had come into her cheeks. 'Yes.' She would have to say more than that, she thought. 'It's just the day for a good walk.' Her motherly instinct overcame her awkwardness. 'You ought not to stand here in the cold... You've got no coat on.'

He smiled again then. 'Then I'll go indoors again, but you must come with me—'

Her 'No, thank you, sir,' was rather sharper than she had intended, but he didn't appear to notice that. 'Then I'll come with you, if I may. The dogs need a run.'

He took her arm, went back to the house and ushered her inside. 'Go into the sitting-room,' he suggested, and opened a door in the wide hall. 'I'll only be a moment.' Katherine waited, trying to overcome her surprise at finding he lived in the very house she had always admired.

He was as good as his word. A moment later he was back again, this time in a thick jacket and accompanied by two golden labradors. There hadn't been enough time to examine the room properly, but she had an impression of warmth and comfort and well-polished furniture.

'Charlie—and this is Flo, and if you find their names peculiar I must explain that one of my small nieces named them.' They went into the hall and he opened the street door. 'Which way were you going?' He glanced at her sensible shoes. 'I usually go past the King's House and then cross into the open ground—the dogs like that.'

She hadn't been that way; even on a gloomy winter's afternoon it was a pleasant walk, and the doctor laid himself out to entertain her. Dodie's spiteful words faded before his friendly, casual talk. She found that she was completely at ease with him and, skilfully led on by his careless questions, told him a good deal more about her life with Henry than she realised.

It was already dusk as they turned back, and almost dark when they reached the house. Katherine bent to pat the dogs. 'I enjoyed our walk, Dr Fitzroy.' Some of the ease she had been feeling had gone, and she was bent on going quickly. 'I...'

She wasn't given the chance to go. 'So did I. Will you share my tea?'

He took her arm and marched her into his house, and an elderly woman came from the back of the hall. She was undoubtedly Mrs Potts' sister, but without the briskness.

'There you are, sir. Tea's in the drawing-room. I'll wipe those dirty paws before they muddy my floors.' She beamed at Katherine. 'I'll have that coat, miss. There's a cloakroom here...' She bustled Katherine across the hall and into a small room, fitted, as far as Katherine could see, with everything a woman could possibly want if she needed to improve her appearance.

Which she undoubtedly did; the cold and wind had given her a fine colour now, but her hair was all over the place. She used the comb laid ready there, cast a critical eye over her appearance, and went back to the hall.

'In here,' called the doctor from a half opened door, and as she reached it he opened it wide. The dogs were already there, sitting before a blazing fire and, curled up on a little stool to one side of the fireplace, was a rather battered-looking cat with a torn ear, and fur in a variety of colours.

'Joseph.' The doctor waved a large hand at the animal.

'Oh, of course—his coat.' She bent to stroke the animal, who purred loudly.

'Have this chair.' He pulled forward a small, velvet-covered armchair. 'Mrs Spooner is bringing tea. I seldom have time for it, but it's one of the nicest meals, don't you think?'

She had a momentary vision of tea in her room; the serviceable brown teapot and pleasant, plain china and a plate of buttered toast. She agreed politely as she took in the delights of the tea table between them. A muffin dish, polished silver glinting in the firelight, wedges of buttered toast spread with what looked like anchovy paste, a plate of little cakes, another with a chocolate sponge oozing cream and, on a silver tray, a silver teapot and milk jug, flanked by delicate china cups and saucers. She could remember, years ago, her mother sitting beside a similar tea table.

The doctor, watching her wistful face, said cheerfully, 'Will you pour, Katherine?' When she had done so, and they had their muffins on their plates, he asked, 'Now, tell me, how do you like your new job?'

'Very much. There's another nursing aide on the ward—Andy—she's been so kind and patient. Sister's very stern, but I expect she has to be. Staff Nurse is kind, too—I don't talk to the student nurses much; I don't go to meals with them and there's no time to talk on the ward.'

'Good. You're not too tired at the end of the day?'

'Just my feet, and they'll be all right once they're used to it. I'm really very happy.'

He passed her the plate of toast and then helped himself. 'And Mrs Potts has made you comfortable?'

'Oh, yes.' She painted an exaggerated picture of the comforts of her room, at the same time aware of the subdued splendour of the room they were sitting in. It was low-ceilinged, with panelled walls hung with portraits and furnished with comfortable chairs, and old, beautifully polished furniture. The curtains had been drawn across the lattice windows, and the crimson brocade reflected the soft light from the table lamps scattered around. Well, she wasn't exactly fibbing, she assured herself, and he would never see her attic, anyway…

They were eating chocolate cake and laughing together about Joseph and the dogs when Katherine heard Mrs Spooner's voice in the hall, and a moment later the door opened and Dodie came in.

She stopped short half-way across the room. 'Well, well—what a picture of cosy domestic bliss!' She gave a little trill of laughter, but her voice had a nasty edge to it. She ignored Katherine and went and sat in a chair close to the doctor. 'Is there any tea left in the pot? I had the absurd notion that you might like to have some company for tea, but I see that you've got it already.'

The doctor had stood up as she went in, but now he sat down again, quite unruffled by the look of fury on her face. 'Katherine and I have had a delightful walk with the dogs.' He paused as his housekeeper came in with fresh tea. 'Any news of your grandparents?'

'Not that I know of.' Dodie shrugged her shoulders prettily. 'You know what old people are; I have an idea they'll be back here again before long. I've heard of a marvellous woman who will live with them.' She glanced at Katherine as though she had just remembered that she was there. 'Bad luck on you, but you've got work, haven't you?'

'How fortunate,' observed Dr Fitzroy smoothly, 'that you've got someone lined up, for Katherine is working at the hospital and doing very well...'

Katherine put down her cup and saucer. 'I'm very happy there,' she said to Dodie as she got to her feet. 'I must go now—thank you for my tea.'

Dr Fitzroy had got up, too; he went to the door with her and leaving it open followed her into the hall. 'Did Mrs Spooner take your coat?' He took it from the housekeeper and helped her on with it. 'A very pleasant afternoon,' he told her in his calm way, 'we must do it again.'

A remark which Katherine put down to a polite piece of nonsense designed to put her at her ease. It had been a lovely few hours—almost, but not quite spoilt by Dodie.

Mrs Potts' kitchen, cosy though it was, seemed something of a let-down after the splendours of the doctor's drawing-room; Katherine joined in the chatter about Christmas while her thoughts were somewhere else. Was Dodie still at his house, she wondered, or were they spending the evening together, dining and dancing? Mrs Potts, repeating her enquiry as to whether Katherine would be working during the Christmas holiday, wondered why she was so dreamy.

'So sorry,' Katherine apologised. 'Yes, I'll be working on Christmas Day and Boxing Day, but I have Christmas Eve off. I don't mind at all, though. It isn't as though I have a family to go to.'

Mrs Potts, who had heard all about Henry from the doctor, said nothing to this; she liked the doctor and she was sorry for Katherine. 'Well, I'll be here,' she said cheerfully. 'Miss Kendall goes home, don't you, dear? But Miss Fish and Mrs Dunster will be here, too. I dare say you'll have a bit of fun at the hospital, Miss Marsh?'

'Oh, I expect so. Mrs Potts, would you mind very much calling me Katherine?'

'Well, now that you ask, I see no reason why I shouldn't. What do they call you at the hospital?'

'Oh, Sister always says Miss Marsh, but everyone else calls me Katherine. Some of the patients call me Katie.'

'Very familiar,' observed Miss Fish severely.

'Not really, they're only being friendly.' Miss Fish looked about to argue the point, so Katherine changed the conversation smartly. 'We have a kind of bran tub for the staff presents on the ward, we each put in something. Has anyone any suggestions as to what I should get?'

The elder ladies had no hesitation in choosing nice white hankies, and Miss Kendall instantly countered that with lacy tights, while Mrs Potts voted for a nice headscarf.

None of these really appealed to Katherine; she wandered round the shops the next morning looking for something she would like to have herself. She found it; a little china vase, white, with violets painted on it. There was no price, but there would be no harm in asking.

She became aware that there was someone standing beside her. 'Christmas shopping?' asked Dr Fitzroy, and she nodded for, as usual, her breath had become really erratic at the sight of him. 'So am I. This, by the way is a young cousin of mine, Edward.'

She saw that there was someone with him. A much younger man, not much older than herself, with a cheerful face which wasn't quite good-looking, a shock of brown hair and an engaging grin.

'This is Katherine,' explained the doctor. 'She came to my help some weeks ago; she now works at the hospital.'

Edward shook hands. 'Nice to meet you. I'm staying over Christmas, perhaps we shall see something of each other.'

'Well, I don't expect so. I'm working...'

'You can't be working all the time?'

She smiled warmly at him. 'No.'

'Good. So we'll have an evening out and I'll tell you my life story.' He looked at the doctor, standing impassively by. 'Do you see a lot of each other?'

Dr Fitzroy and Katherine exchanged a glance. 'Hardly,' said the doctor, 'but I'm sure I can manage to convey any message you might wish to send.'

'I could phone,' said Edward airily.

'Oh, no, you couldn't!' The look of horror on Katherine's face brought him up short. 'Sister doesn't allow phone calls.'

'Old dragon, is she? Just goes to show what happens to nurses if they stay long enough in hospital.'

Katherine went pink. 'Oh, but I'm not a nurse. I'm only an aide; that's between a ward maid and a new student nurse who doesn't know anything.'

Edward was unimpressed. 'Oh, good, you'll not get the chance to turn into a dragon.' He caught the doctor's glance and added, 'Oh, all right, Jason, I know you've no time to dally.'

They bade her goodbye, Edward with the declared intention of seeing her again, Dr Fitzroy with grave friendliness.

She stood there, where they had left her, thinking in a muddled way that it was the greatest of pities that Edward seemed to have taken to her at once, and Dr Fitzroy treated her with an impersonal courtesy which she found most unsatisfactory. She quite forgot about the vase, and wandered along, stopping here and there to appraise some particularly eye-catching garment; eye-catching in the sense that it would attract the doctor's eye—a piece of nonsense actually, for it would take several weeks' wages to pay for any one of them.

The spirit of Christmas was beginning to pervade the ward when she went back on duty the next day. Those patients who weren't actually flat on their backs were pressed into making paper flowers, paper chains and coloured crêpe-paper mats for the bed tables and locker tops. They would be the very devil to keep tidy and clean, observed Andy, but Sister, who considered herself artistic, always got carried away at Christmas.

'Had you ever thought of training as a nurse?' Andy asked Katherine as they made up empty beds. 'Me, I'd be no good, haven't even got O-levels, but I bet you've been to a good school.'

Katherine mitred a corner neatly. 'Oh, I don't think I'd do at all. I stayed home with my mother when I left school, and then I went to live with my brother and his wife for two years.'

'What did you do there? General dogsbody?'

'Well, yes, I suppose I was.'

'Then how did you escape, even if it's hardly a bed of roses here?'

Katherine explained, and when she had finished Andy said, 'Lord, what a bit of luck for you! And Dr Fitzroy's such a duck of a man...' She caught sight of Katherine's face and said quickly, 'Have you been to see your brother since you came here?'

'No, but I thought I'd go on my next days off; just to say hello—I wouldn't stay.'

'When Bill's away, you and I will have an afternoon off together if we can fix it.' Bill was her fiancé, a plumber by trade, who occasionally worked away from Salisbury. 'He's home for Christmas, and I've got Boxing Day off, so I'll go to his place and then he will come home with me.'

'That'll be nice.' Katherine sounded cheerful and thanked heaven that she was working over Christmas. On Christmas Eve she would be free to go into the city and mix with the crowds and feel part of them for a while, and she would be able to go to the midnight service. Everyone said that Christmas on the wards was quite fun...

The ward was quite busy: irascible old men with bronchitis and heart failure adding to the hazards of hernia repairs, duodenal ulcers and colostomies, and a sprinkling of younger ones with appendicitis, nasty injuries from their work or a car accident. Whether they liked it or not, Sister had them all working on Christmas decorations, so Katherine and Andy were in constant demand to give a hand, for the student nurses were too busy learning from their seniors, and they in turn were too busy with dressings and medicine rounds and all the complicated paraphernalia Katherine only half understood. The week went by with no sign of Dr Fitzroy; he seldom came on to the surgical side, but usually she caught a glimpse of him as she did errands to the various departments. Her days off came round once more and she decided she would pay her brother a visit; it was, after all, almost Christmas, and a season of good will.

She set off by bus in the afternoon, bearing small gifts and wearing her new coat and a neat corduroy hat to match it. It was a cold day, but the sun shone fitfully, and she was warmed by the knowledge that there was a week's wages in her purse. Even after paying the rent, there was money over—not much, but more than she had had for a long time.

She could hear the children shouting and screaming as she went up the garden path and, as she knocked on the door, Joyce's voice raised in anger. No one came to the door, so she knocked again, and this time Joyce answered it. 'What do you want?' she wanted to know snappily. 'Don't think you're coming back!'

'No. I don't think that. I brought your Christmas presents. May I come in?'

'I suppose so.' Joyce stood aside for her to go into the hall, and it was at once evident that Mrs Todd hadn't felt like doing the floors for some time, let alone a little dusting. The sitting-room was in a like state. Katherine itched to get her hands on the hoover and a couple of dusters, but it wasn't her business any more.

'Well,' said Joyce, 'let's have these presents. I can't stop to entertain you, I'm busy.'

'Could I see the children?'

Joyce shrugged. 'If you want to. A girl comes to look after them in the mornings, but I have to see to them when she goes home.' She shot Katherine a furious look. 'Thanks to you and your ingratitude.'

Katherine ignored that; she hadn't come to quarrel. She said reasonably, 'They're in the nursery? I'll go along...'

'Do. Don't stay long.'

They weren't particularly pleased to see her, but took their presents without thanks and tore off the wrappings. She had been silly to come, reflected Katherine, but all the same she felt sorry for the pair; they looked uncared-for and grubby, although healthy enough. She bade them an unheeded goodbye and went back to Joyce.

'I won't keep you, Katherine, and there's no point in you being here; Henry won't want to see you.' She studied Katherine's clothes. 'Still working, I suppose?'

'Yes.' She didn't tell Joyce that she had left the Graingers; she wouldn't be interested anyway. She had been stupid to come. 'I hope you all have a happy Christmas,' she said politely as Joyce urged her towards the door.

In the brief half-hour she had been indoors, the weather had changed: the sun had gone for good and the wind was biting. There was no bus for an hour and nowhere she could stay. She walked briskly down to the gate, and heard the door slam behind her. She would start walking. Luckily, she was wearing sensible shoes…

It was several miles until the road she was on joined the main road at Wilton; there would be a good chance of picking up a bus there. She quickened her pace; the sky was lowering and dusk wasn't far off. She had gone a mile or more when Dr Fitzroy's Bentley passed her, going the other way. He had been driving quite fast and she didn't think he had seen her. In any case, he was going in the opposite direction. She walked on, thinking about him; indeed, he occupied her thoughts incessantly.

The Bentley drew up beside her almost without a sound. 'Hop in quickly, I'm on the wrong side of the road,' advised the doctor, leaning over to open the door for her. When she was sitting beside him, he asked, 'Did you miss the bus?'

She shook her head; it was absurd that now that she was being driven back in comfort the desire to weep was overwhelming. The doctor cast her a swift glance—two tears were trickling down her cheeks.

He said with brisk friendliness, 'I'm just going home for tea. Do come and keep me company.'

She found her voice. 'You were going the other way.'

'Nothing important.' He went on cheerfully, 'How is the work going? Not too much for you? Edward will be at home, which is a good thing, for he intended coming round to see you this evening.'

Katherine sniffed, blew her prosaic little nose and said, 'How nice…'

'He's a good lad,' observed her companion easily, 'and looking forward to seeing something of you while he's here.'

They were through Wilton and going fast along the road into Salisbury. It was almost dark now, but the first of the evening traffic had hardly got started. The doctor turned away from the city centre before they reached it, and took a series of small roads which brought him very close to his house. There were lights shining from the ground-floor windows as he stopped the car outside his front door, got out and opened Katherine's door for her, and by the time they had crossed the pavement Mrs Spooner was waiting for them. Katherine let out a little sigh of contentment as she entered the hall. The house welcomed her, and Edward's cheerful face peering round the drawing-room door made the welcome even warmer.

CHAPTER SIX

EDWARD crossed the hall, flatteringly pleased to see her, and she had a moment's regret that he wasn't Dr Fitzroy, but in such thoughts lay an unhappiness she must avoid at all costs. She returned his exuberant greeting with a warm one of her own, while the doctor stood quietly watching them both.

'Let me have your coat,' he said softly. 'Mrs Spooner will bring tea.'

He let Edward do most of the talking as they had their tea, and presently excused himself on the plea of work, and went away to his study, leaving Edward detailing his life at the London hospital where he was a junior houseman.

Katherine listened and laughed and wished that the doctor would return. Perversely, when he did, she declared that she would have to dash, but not before accepting Edward's pressing invitation to have dinner with him on the following evening. What was more, he declared that he would walk back with her to Mrs Potts' house, so they set off presently, seen on their way by a strangely avuncular doctor. It was as though he had raised an invisible barrier between them, thought Katherine, walking briskly through the streets beside Edward. There always had been a barrier, she admitted to herself, but now suddenly he had turned

into a much older man, prepared to be amused at their
youthful chatter, but not wishing to be part of it. And
yet he wasn't old—not even middle-aged...

Her wandering thoughts ceased abruptly when Edward, who had been rambling on about a nurse on
night duty who had caught his fancy, said, 'Jason's a
splendid chap, isn't he? A pity if he lets that Dodie
get her claws into him. She's a smasher, I grant you,
but sheer poison to a man like him.'

'Why?'

'My dear girl, all she thinks about is clothes and
having a good time and spending money. Can't think
what he sees in her...'

Katherine agreed with him, only silently; Dr Fitzroy needed a loving wife, one who would look after
him and be his companion and let him get on with
his work when he wanted to, but be there when he
wanted her. She herself would be exactly right, but
there were a number of drawbacks. She was what
Joyce called homely; moreover, unlike a girl who had
the means, she had none with which to disguise the
homeliness. She didn't move in his circle, either, nor
did she see any likelihood of ever doing so.

She parted from Edward at Mrs Potts' front door,
promising to be ready when he called the following
evening at seven o'clock. He gave her a brotherly
hug, wished her a cheerful goodnight and strode off.
A nice boy, she earnestly reflected, shutting the front
door carefully behind her. Such a pity that her brother
couldn't have been more like him.

Edward had suggested that they go to the Rose and

Crown for dinner, a well-known hotel dating back some few hundred years, where the food was excellent and the service likewise, and where Katherine's one and only wool dress would pass muster. She went to bed well content, if a little wistful at the doctor's impersonal attitude towards her. It was just as well she wasn't at his house to overhear the conversation he had with his cousin.

Dr Fitzroy had listened to Edward's plans for the following evening. 'Nice little thing,' concluded that young man. 'A bit behind the times, though. Led a sheltered life, probably.'

The doctor was pouring drinks. 'Probably,' he agreed casually, 'and not much money to spend, so don't take her anywhere too dressy.'

'Why doesn't she do her training?'

'I think that probably she might do that once she has some self-confidence. She has been living with a rather overbearing brother and his wife.'

'Needs a jolt, does she?'

The doctor shook his head. 'A series of gentle prods, I think.' He went and sat down in his chair by the fire. 'I'm taking Dodie to a carol concert after dinner. Will you be able to amuse yourself?'

Christmas, vaguely distant, was suddenly there; Katherine helped hang chains of bright-coloured paper on the ward, arranged posies of paper flowers at the foot of each patient's bed, and assembled a series of paper hats for everyone to wear. It was hard work, but she enjoyed it; her evening out with Edward had done her a lot of good; it was pleasant to feel that someone liked her enough to take her out to dinner, besides she thought he was an amusing companion and treated her with the ease of a brother. He was full of good advice, too; she should start her training as a nurse, he counselled her, and get herself a secure future.

'I'm sure you'll get married,' he had told her airily, 'but you can't be sure of that, can you?' And, when she agreed, he added, 'Once you're trained, you could afford a small flat of your own, and get out and about a bit. Of course, it would take a few years, but you're still young enough.'

She had laughed then, but afterwards such a prospect looked bleak and lonely. Still, it would be better than being an aide. She had promised him that she would consider it.

Take-in week started a couple of days before Christmas and, as was only to be expected, the ward filled rapidly with victims of road accidents, those who had anticipated the festive season rather too soon and got themselves drunk enough to fall about and cut themselves on broken glass, or knocked themselves out against doors they thought were open and weren't. Over and above these were the normal quota of ulcers and hernias and appendices. Sister, not to be thwarted from her Christmas celebrations, moved the ill patients to one end of the ward, and chivvied the porters to hang holly wherever there was space for it.

Mrs Potts had done her best too, with a tree in the sitting-room window, lit at dusk, and the curtains undrawn so that the passers-by could enjoy it. There were mince pies at supper, too, and the promise of turkey on Christmas Day. Katherine was assured that hers would be kept hot in the oven until such time as she got back from the hospital.

Several of the nurses had Christmas leave, so her days off had been split: Christmas Eve and the day after Boxing Day, an arrangement which suited her very well. It would be cheerful on the ward, and there was the joy of knowing that she would have plenty to do. The prospect of spending Christmas Day in the company of Mrs Dunster and Miss Fish was daunting, and on Boxing Day Mrs Potts was going to spend the morning with her sister, Mrs Spooner.

The weather had turned very cold, with the prospect of snow. Katherine was about early on Christmas Eve, intent on enjoying the bustle in the shops. And since she had some money in her pocket she intended to have her lunch out, and should she see a pretty dress she would buy it. Edward had suggested that they might have another evening out before he left Salisbury...

The streets were already full of shoppers. Recklessly, she treated herself to coffee at Snell's, sitting lonely amid cheerful family parties and well-dressed matrons comparing shopping lists. Presently, she began her round of the shops. It had begun to snow, and the shops had turned on their lights. She went from one window to the other, choosing what she would buy if ever she had enough money. There were several boutiques where she might find a dress; she went to each of them in turn, searching for something she would be able to wear on any of the likely occasions when she might need to dress up a little. There weren't likely to be many of them, but the wool dress was no longer good enough; besides, she was sick to death of it. She finally decided on a fine wool crêpe dress, paisley patterned in several shades of amber and dark green. It was plain, but it fitted her well, and the price was right. Well satisfied with her purchase, she had coffee and a sandwich at a snack bar, and combed the cheaper shops for shoes to go with the dress. She found these too—plain black leather, because she would be able to wear them with the few clothes she had, but they were high-heeled and suited her small feet.

Well pleased with herself, she bought crumpets for her tea and went back through the snow to her room, where she lit the gas fire, drew the curtains and toasted the crumpets. When she had had her tea she tried on the dress and shoes, craning her neck to see as much as possible of herself in the looking-glass, before putting them away and getting into the wool dress again, and going down to supper. Miss Kendall had gone, and Miss Fish and Mrs Dunster were hardly in a festive mood, but Mrs Potts produced boiled ham and parsley sauce, with coffee to follow and, since it was Christmas, mince tarts. After the two elderly ladies had gone back to their rooms, Katherine stayed behind and helped Mrs Potts with the dishes and told her about the new dress over a second cup of coffee.

'A shame you have to work on Christmas Day,'

declared Mrs Potts. 'It didn't ought to be allowed. There'll be a drop of hot soup for you on the stove when you get back from the cathedral. And mind you get straight to bed—it'll be late enough.'

Katherine thanked her and agreed meekly, although what she was supposed to do to keep her out of her bed at that hour of night was beyond her. She went back to her room and laid the small gifts she had for Mrs Potts and her fellow lodgers ready on the table, and then sat down by the fire to read until it was time to go to the midnight service. She didn't read for long though. She had barely glimpsed Dr Fitzroy during the previous week, but that didn't stop her thinking about him.

The snow had stopped by the time she left the house, but it lay thick on the pavements and garden walls along the side streets she walked through. The close was a vast white blanket, its paths already filled with those going to the cathedral, which was already almost full. Katherine found a seat to one side, close to the medieval clock, hemmed in by an old gentleman in a hairy tweed suit, with a resounding cough, and a haughty matron who overflowed on to Katherine's chair. Not that she minded; there was a distinct feeling of goodwill and a happy peacefulness all around her, so it was impossible to feel lonely.

It was long past midnight as she made her way through the crowds leaving the cathedral, and she started off briskly along the snowy path towards North Gate, prudently keeping to the main streets. She was almost at the Gate when she was brought to an abrupt halt by Dr Fitzroy's voice.

'I thought I saw you as we left the Cathedral. Come back and have a warm drink before you go to bed?' He had put a hand on her arm, and she saw that Edward was on the other side of her, and Dodie, looking furious, was just behind him.

She stammered a little, her heart thumping with the delight of seeing him. 'Oh—thank you, but I must get back. I'm on duty in the morning...'

She found herself turned round and walked smartly away from the High Street, in the direction of the doctor's house. 'All the more reason why you should enjoy a few minutes of Christmas now. I'll take you back, and at this hour half an hour more or less isn't going to make much difference.'

Edward had taken her other arm and the four of them walked arm-in-arm, the two men talking trivialities, deliberately setting out to make her laugh, while Dodie walked sullenly along. At the house, Mrs Spooner had the door open before they reached it, and in a flurry of good wishes and cheerful talk Katherine was ushered into the drawing-room. There was a roaring fire, with Charlie and Flo and Joseph lying side by side before it, and the table in the window was laden with several covered dishes, a small Christmas tree, bristling with lights and baubles, and a tray of drinks.

The doctor had taken Katherine's coat and urged her to sit down near the fire, and presently Mrs Spooner came in with a steaming jug.

'Hot chocolate,' she declared. 'Just right after that walk back. And there's sausage rolls and smoked salmon and mince pies on the table.' She looked at the doctor. 'Will you see to the wine, Doctor?'

Edward had sat down beside Katherine and handed her a plate of food; Dodie had flung herself down on one of the sofas, declaring that she couldn't eat a morsel and would someone give her a drink? She didn't speak to Katherine at all, but her silence went almost unnoticed, for Mrs Spooner was handing round cups of chocolate and the doctor was filling glasses, keeping up a flow of small talk.

He brought a glass over to Katherine and said kindly, 'We shall have a party on New Year's Eve. Edward will be here, and he'd like you to come— he's scared to ask you, in case you refuse.'

Katherine bit into a mince pie. 'Why should I do that?' she asked in surprise. 'Oh, you mean if I'm on duty! Well, I'm not and I should love to come, thank you very much.' She added anxiously, 'Will it be a grand affair?'

Dodie answered her. 'You mean black ties? Of course it will. You'll have to mortgage your wages for weeks and buy something presentable—or not come.'

Both men looked at her. 'I say...' began Edward, but the doctor cut in, 'We'll forgive you for that silly joke, Dodie, since it's Christmas. I shouldn't drink any more if I were you.'

He sounded perfectly good-natured, but there was a tinge of ice in his pleasant voice, so that Dodie

mumbled, 'Oh, can't anyone take a joke any more?'
She got up, and with a defiant look at him, went to
the table and refilled her glass.

The doctor took no notice, but sat down on the
other side of the hearth and engaged Katherine in a
gentle conversation which lasted until she had finished her chocolate, drunk a glass of champagne as a
toast to Christmas and suggested quietly and a little
hesitantly that she should go back to Mrs Potts. He
didn't attempt to dissuade her; she wished Dodie
goodnight and the compliments of the season, received a brotherly hug for Christmas from Edward
and got into the doctor's car.

It was only a few minutes' drive; he drew up outside Mrs Potts' house and got out with her. 'I have a
key,' said Katherine. 'Please don't bother...'

He took the key from her and opened the door,
switched on the hall light and stood looking down at
her. 'A very pleasant start to Christmas,' he observed,
and watched the colour creep into her cheeks. 'And,
I hope, a happy one for you, Katherine.' He bent and
kissed her cheek, pushed her gently into the hall and
closed the door. She stood listening to him driving
away, and after a minute or two switched off the light
and went upstairs to her room.

Her room was cold; she put the kettle on the gas
ring and filled her hot-water bottle, then jumped into
bed and with her chilly person curled around its
warmth, was asleep before she could put two thoughts
together.

It was still pitch dark when the alarm wakened her.

She lit the gas fire, crept down to the bathroom and dressed rapidly before sitting by its warmth to eat her breakfast. There had been more snow in the night, bringing with it a stillness made even more apparent by the lack of early morning traffic, and when she let herself quietly out of the house her feet sank into white crispness. It seemed a pity to spoil it with footprints.

The hospital was humming with subdued activity, its windows lit, a kind of background buzz betraying the readying of patients before breakfast, trollies being wheeled round the wards, and the never ending toing and froing of the nurses. Katherine hurried to the changing room and five minutes later made her way to the surgical wing. To save time, she took a short-cut past the theatre block, nipping along smartly, secure in the knowledge that at that early hour there would be no ward sisters to eye her with suspicion or question her speed. She was level with the heavy swing doors which separated the theatres from the main corridors when they were flung open and Dr Fitzroy came out. He was immaculate; she had never seen him otherwise, but he was the last person she expected to see. She came to a slithering halt staring at him.

'Hello again, Katherine.'

He grinned at her from a tired face and she found her voice. 'Haven't you been to bed?' she asked in a shocked voice. 'Have you been here all night?'

'No, to the first question, yes, to the second.' He

was standing idly beside her, and for the moment she
had forgotten all about going on duty.

She said urgently, 'I hope you're going home now.'
Her loving eyes searched his face. 'You're tired. You
need a good breakfast and then a nap...'

The slight lift of his eyebrows sent the colour rush-
ing to her face. She stammered, 'I'm late...' and almost ran from him. What a fool he must think her to
be! She felt near to tears as she reached the ward, and
Staff Nurse, on the point of telling her that she was
almost five minutes late on duty, changed her mind;
Katherine was a hard worker and didn't watch the
clock, and after all it *was* Christmas Day.

Despite Sister's efforts to send home as many people as possible so that they might enjoy the festive
season at home with their families, the ward had filled
up. The student nurse with whom she was making
beds gave her a quick résumé of the admissions during her day off and added, 'There was a bit of a flap
on during the night, too—there were three RTAs—
we got two of them, the other man died in the theatre.
They called in Dr Fitzroy just after two o'clock, but
the junior night nurse told me that after five hours
they had to admit defeat.'

They smoothed the counterpane of the empty bed
and turned to the next one, occupied by a middle-
aged man who had had a gastrectomy three days pre-
viously, and was beginning to feel himself again.
There was no chance to carry on their talk; he wished
them a happy Christmas and they made silly little
jokes about his diet while they made his bed. After

that, Katherine went off to the sluice, and presently to the kitchen to help with the morning drinks.

The ward was in festive mood, even Sister had unbent sufficiently to wish everyone a happy Christmas and take part in the drawing of gifts from the bran tub in her office. Katherine, being the newest member of the staff, and also the most lowly, was last, which meant that there was no choice. She fished around and unearthed a small, flat packet; notelets—so useful, Staff Nurse pointed out kindly, for writing thank-you notes for presents.

Only Katherine hadn't had any presents.

The patients' dinner was the high spot of the day; the consultant surgeon, Mr Bracewaite, arrived with the turkey and, suitably aproned and crowned with a chef's cap, carved with the same precision he exhibited in the theatre. Katherine, trotting to and fro with plates, sitting patients up, cutting up food for those who weren't able to do so for themselves, kept out of his way. He had a reputation for being peppery and ill-tempered, and rarely spoke to anyone less senior than a ward sister, or, if he had to, a staff nurse. He did a hurried round after he had carved the turkey, and then went away to Sister's office to drink a glass of the excellent sherry he gave her each Christmas. With the disappearance of authority, the ward took on a festive air: crackers were pulled, paper hats were donned and the nurses took it in turns to go to the kitchen and pick bits off the turkey carcass. But this pleasant state of affairs didn't last long; Mr Bracewaite went away, and Sister summoned the two staff nurses and the senior of the student nurses into the office to eat their own lunch—sausage rolls and mince pies and a selection of sandwiches with a bottle of plonk. By the time it was Katherine's turn she was famished but, since it was time to settle the patients for their brief afternoon rest, she had to gobble her food and then rush round taking away pillows, filling water jugs and fetching and carrying for Sister and Staff Nurse. She was surprised when Sister told her that she might take an hour off so that she might tour the hospital and visit the other wards. Her companion was the most junior of the student nurses, a pretty girl who, once they were out of the ward, caught Katherine by the hand. 'There's someone I'm going to see,' she told her, her eyes sparkling. 'He's in the residents' wing, and if anyone wants to know, tell them I was with you all the time.'

She dashed away, leaving Katherine open-mouthed. The residents' flats had been pointed out to her when she first arrived; no one went there, she had been told sternly. If they did, the consequences would be dire. She watched the tail end of her companion disappearing along the corridor and then set out on her own.

She went to the medical wards, hopeful that she might see Dr Fitzroy, but he wasn't there. Common sense had told her that he wouldn't be. She went rather shyly round the ward, accepted a glass of something from a friendly nurse, and went along to the orthopaedic wards where she exchanged greetings with the numerous owners of broken limbs, and drank another glass of something in Sister's office. Then she made her way to ENT, where she ate a mince pie, before opening the swing doors into the children's ward.

She had no idea what she had been drinking, but whatever she had been offered mixed into a pleasant glow in her insides, making her feel remarkably carefree. She started down the ward, another mince pie in her hand, stopping to talk to the toddlers in their cots. She was at the end when she saw Dr Fitzroy sitting on one of the small beds, a baby tucked under one arm.

With sorrowful hindsight, much later, Katherine realised that it was the variety of drinks which had loosened her tongue so deplorably, but at that moment she didn't give it much thought. She advanced and said happily, 'Oh, hello, Jason. Shouldn't you be in bed?'

She smiled widely at him and he laughed a little, his eyes gleaming with amusement. 'Oh, but I had to carve the turkey, you know.' He upended the baby so that it faced her. 'See who this is? Our foundling, no less. Growing up into a splendid lad.'

She sat down beside him and took the baby from him. 'He's gorgeous. Has he been christened?'

'Oh, yes—Noel. It couldn't be anything else, could it?'

She tickled the baby under its chin and it smiled widely and windily. 'Did anyone find out who is the mother?'

'No, I'm afraid not.' He took the baby and put him

tidily into his cot. 'Are you enjoying your Christmas?'

'Oh, yes, thank you, Dr Fitzroy.'

'You called me Jason. I rather liked that.'

She went very pink. 'Oh, I'm sorry, I can't think why…that is, I've been given quite a lot to drink…so silly of me.' She stood up quickly and went on breathlessly, 'I hope you have a lovely evening when you get home! I must go, Sister said an hour.'

She went quickly down the ward and out of the doors at the far end, and he watched her small, neat figure dwindling. Almost pretty, he reflected, with those eyes, and now she had filled out with Mrs Potts' wholesome cooking.

It had been a long day, reflected Katherine, going back home through the snow, but she had enjoyed it, all except that last bit when she had met Dr Fitzroy. What a good thing she almost never saw him these days!

Mrs Potts was waiting for her; Miss Fish and Mrs Dunster had retired to their rooms, Christmas or no Christmas, but her landlady had set the table in the kitchen with a holly centrepiece and crackers, and within ten minutes had produced roast turkey and all the trimmings, urged Katherine to sit down and eat it, and sat down opposite to her. 'I reckon you had a busy day,' she invited, and listened while Katherine, between mouthfuls, told of her doings.

'And you're on duty again tomorrow? I call it a shame…'

'I don't mind a bit, Mrs Potts. It isn't as though I

have anywhere to go, and the next day I'm free, anyway.'

She started on her pudding, suddenly sleepy, so that she was glad when Mrs Potts offered her a cup of coffee. 'When you've finished, you can have a bath and jump right into bed,' she told her comfortably.

Which was exactly what Katherine did, to fall asleep at once and dreamlessly.

She hadn't expected to get any off duty the next day, so it came as a pleasant surprise when, just after four o'clock, after the last of the visitors who had come for Boxing Day tea on the wards had gone, she was told by Sister that she might go off for the evening. 'You have worked very well,' conceded that lady, 'and it is your day off tomorrow.' She nodded dismissal and Katherine skipped away, intent on getting out of the hospital before some disastrous happening should prevent her leaving.

Usually she came and went through the car park at the back of the hospital and a series of small streets, but there would be little traffic and the main streets were bright with decorations and lights, a small sop to her unconscious wish to be part of the Christmas scene. She pushed the heavy door open and crossed the courtyard, packed with cars, and made for the street, planning her day off as she went. There was no point in getting up too early, so she would enjoy the rare pleasure of breakfast in bed and then go for a walk. She reviewed the areas as far away from Dr Fitzroy's house as possible, and decided that she might walk to Alderbury, three miles away to the south-east of Salisbury, remembering going there years ago when her father was alive. There was an inn there, she would treat herself to a snack lunch and walk back to have her tea by the fire... She hadn't noticed Dr Fitzroy's car creep up beside her and stop.

He wound down the window. 'Off duty? So am I— hop in and come and have some tea.' He looked at her tired face. 'You can curl up by the fire and go to sleep if you want to.' He had leant across and opened the door for her, and with only the faintest of objections she got in beside him. To be with him, even for half an hour, would be heaven, made even more heavenly by the prospect of tea. She said in her calm little voice, 'Do you have to work on Boxing Day, too?'

'Only when I need to—I shall make up for it by having a day off tomorrow. Edward will be leaving in a few days; if the weather's good I think I might drive him over to Stourhead, it should be looking splendid in the snow.'

'Does he plan to stay in London?'

'Only until such time as he needs to get some experience. He wants to be a GP eventually, in this part of the world.'

The doctor drew up in front of his house and got out to help her plough through the snow which the wind had piled into small drifts along the pavement. He unlocked his front door and urged her inside to pleasant warmth and comfort and Edward's pleased welcome, dogs barking and Mrs Spooner coming silently to lead Katherine away to tidy herself.

They had tea round the fire, muffins and rich fruitcake and featherlight scones with butter, while Edward talked. He was a great talker, and an amusing one, too; the doctor sat in his huge chair, the dogs at his feet, and encouraged Edward gently so that presently Katherine was laughing at his outrageous stories and feeling very much at her ease.

A happy state of affairs which wasn't to last. Katherine, invited to go to Stourhead on the following day, had just said a breathless, delighted 'yes' when Dodie joined them.

She made a delightful picture when she paused in the open doorway. 'I crept in without bothering Mrs Spooner—you really should lock your door, Jason...' She paused as her eyes alighted on Katherine. She turned a shoulder to her without speaking, and addressed the doctor.

'I'm sorry, darling, I've been persuaded to go with the Crofts to Winchester for lunch, but will you come and fetch me afterwards? We could go out to dinner...' She smiled beguilingly. 'Naughty me to stand you up—I know I did promise to keep tomorrow free.'

The doctor spoke blandly, without any trace of annoyance. 'Never mind, Dodie, as it happens I'm taking Edward and Katherine over to Stourhead. It's ideal weather for a walk there, and the dogs need a good run.'

Her beautiful eyes narrowed. 'Supposing I had refused the Crofts?'

'Then you could have come, too—a pleasant foursome. You can always change your mind.'

'I can think of nothing more dreary then plodding round Stourhead at this time of the year.' She was in a real temper now, and Katherine looked at the doctor to see what he would do.

Nothing. He looked positively placid, and after a few fuming moments Dodie changed her tactics. 'Well, darling, let's go to town at the weekend and see a show and dance somewhere. I've quite made up my mind—I've got a gorgeous dress I'm simply longing to wear.'

'Can't be done, I'm afraid. I've two consultations on Saturday, and there's a committee meeting on Sunday morning.'

'In that case, there's no point in staying here listening to your excuses. I've no doubt you'll find amusement enough while I'm away.'

Her smouldering eyes turned to Katherine, still sitting there, trying to look as though she was miles away.

'You know, you should do something about your make-up and go to a decent hairdresser. You're a complete nonentity!'

She swept from the room before anyone could speak.

The silence which followed seemed like an eternity to Katherine although it was barely a couple of minutes. 'I'm sorry about that, Katherine,' said the doctor. 'Dodie gets quite worked up, and says things she doesn't mean.'

Edward joined in, anxious to make light of Dodie's rudeness. 'Always was a nasty, rude child,' he observed. 'I suppose I've known her for so long that we don't bother overmuch.'

Katherine looked at their concerned faces. 'It's perfectly all right,' she said to them calmly. 'Dodie was disappointed, and it made her cross. And I've never had any pretensions to good looks. She's quite right, I dare say I could do a lot by way of improvement. It might be a good New Year's resolution.'

'You're perfectly all right as you are,' declared the doctor, which perhaps was an unfortunate remark to make.

'Beyond help,' reflected Katherine ruefully. All the same, it would be rather fun to go to a beauty salon and have a professional make-up and her hair done elegantly—perhaps tinted...

'What are you brooding about?' Edward wanted to know.

'I was wondering,' she said composedly, 'if it might be a good idea to have my hair tinted?'

'God forbid!' exploded the doctor, so sharply that she looked at him in surprise.

'It wouldn't suit you,' he said hastily. He was looking remote and saying little; he probably had plans for his evening and wanted her gone.

She got to her feet, saying, 'I really must go—thank you for a lovely tea...'

The two men were standing, one each side of her. 'If you would stay for dinner, we might have a game of poker,' suggested the doctor to her surprise.

'But I don't know how to play.'

'All the better! Edward and I will enjoy teaching

you...' He didn't wait for her to agree, but reached for the phone. 'I'll let Mrs Potts know.'

Rather high-handed, thought Katherine, agog with delight at the thought of an evening spent in his company, and Edward's, of course.

Mrs Spooner came to take away the tea things, received the news that Katherine would be spending the evening, set a tray of drinks ready and went away again, and the three of them settled down to the intricacies of poker. Katherine picked it up quickly, and did so well that Edward remarked, 'You wouldn't know to look at her that Katherine was a gambler at heart, would you?'

'Appearances can be deceptive,' agreed the doctor gravely, 'and sometimes a gamble is worth risking.'

They had dinner presently; Mrs Spooner's home-made chicken soup, Dover sole and fluffy baked potatoes swimming in butter, and a trifle the like of which Katherine hadn't seen, let alone eaten, for many years. Edward wanted to play poker again when they had had their coffee, but she had no wish to outstay her welcome. She was driven back by the doctor, who made no effort to keep her. He wished her a brisk goodnight on Mrs Potts' doorstep.

'We'll fetch you about eleven o'clock,' he said as he put her key in the lock. 'Wear sensible shoes.'

All her shoes were sensible, but there was no point in saying so. She wished him goodnight, thanked him for her pleasant evening and went indoors. Mrs Potts was waiting for her.

'Now, what do you think of that?' she wanted to

know. 'Having a lovely evening with the doctor and that Mr Edward! You got a bit of Christmas, after all.'

Katherine, a kind girl, could see that Mrs Potts was bored with her own company; she sat down and accepted a cup of tea and gave a blow-by-blow account of her evening. 'And I'm going to Stourhead tomorrow,' she finished as she bade her landlady goodnight and danced up to her attic.

CHAPTER SEVEN

KATHERINE woke early, and lay for a while debating with herself what she should wear. She hadn't much choice, but she regretfully ruled out the new dress and her hat; both would look silly at Stourhead. She wished that she had good leather boots, well-cut slacks and a new quilted jacket, but she hadn't. While she ate her breakfast, she puzzled over the problem, counted the money in her purse, tidied her room and went out. Her shoes were low-heeled lace-ups and sensible enough, her slacks were old, but she was a neat girl and they looked well-cared for. Her head buzzing with possibilities, she went to shop. Ten minutes later she came out again, having laid out her money on a woolly cap, gloves and a scarf in holly-berry-red. Her slacks and quilted jacket were in a serviceable dark blue, and she had prudently added thick woollen knee socks to her purchases. She hurried back to try on everything, and the result pleased her well enough; the cap and scarf certainly did a lot to disguise the shabbiness of her slacks and jacket.

She sat down to wait, wondering if they would return before lunch, and decided that it would be more than likely. An hour's brisk walk round the lake would take them to one o'clock, if you counted in the driving to and fro. She began to plan her afternoon, anxious to make the most of her day off.

She didn't get very far with this, for Mrs Potts called up to say that the doctor was waiting for her. She ran downstairs and felt a faint disappointment that it was Edward standing in the hall and not Jason. And she must stop thinking of him as Jason...

Edward greeted her with a friendly warmth and the remark that he was glad to see that, unlike some girls he knew, she was sensibly dressed for outdoor exercise. They called goodbye to Mrs Potts and went out to the car, to find the doctor sitting behind the wheel, looking placid.

'You'd both better get in the back—that's if you don't mind the dogs!' His eyes swept over Katherine and he added, 'Good—you're sensibly turned out.' This remark did nothing for her ego, although upon reflection she supposed that she might take it as a compliment of a sort.

Edward was in fine form, talking nonsense to make her laugh, while the dogs lolled over their feet; but the doctor had little to say, which wasn't surprising really, since the road, although cleared of snow, was icy. But they could drive the whole way on good roads, only for the last mile or so would the snow still be lying. They stopped at Fovant, a village halfway between Salisbury and Shaftesbury, and had coffee at the pub there, and then they drove on again. The sun had struggled through the clouds, and the snow sparkled around them, deep and untouched on the hills, turning the cottages alongside the road into fairy-tale dwellings.

They went out of Shaftesbury on the Gillingham road, and found that it had been more or less cleared, but when they turned off for Stourhead the country lane was packed with snow and the doctor slowed down, going past the row of cottages at the start of the small village, then down the hill towards the entrance to the park, to turn into the yard of the Spread Eagle Inn. He stopped and turned to look at Edward and Katherine.

'Walk first?' he asked. 'That should bring us nicely to one o'clock or thereabouts; the bar will be open until two, so we have plenty of time.'

They all got out and the dogs were put on their leads. 'See about the tickets, will you, Edward?' The doctor was busy with the dogs. 'We'll follow you.'

He took his time putting the dogs on a double lead, and Edward had gone through the gate to the little rustic kiosk where he could get tickets before they were ready to follow him. 'You like Edward?' The doctor's voice was casual.

'Oh, yes—very much—I wish my brother were half such fun, but of course he's a lot older. Thirty-six.'

'The same as myself,' observed the doctor. Katherine gave an agitated little skip beside him and went the colour of her knitted cap. 'Oh, I didn't mean—that is, you don't seem old at all...'

'But past my first exuberant youth? Edward is a mere twenty-four.'

'Yes, he told me.'

'He will be down again for the odd weekend, so you will be able to see something of each other.'

'That will be nice,' Katherine said politely, and wished they they would talk about someone else—the doctor, for instance. She ast about in her head for the best way of introducing this enthralling subject, but by then they had caught up with Edward.

He tucked an arm into hers. 'I say, this is a super spot! I've not been during the winter, I had no idea that it was so magnificent. We ought to have brought some bread for the ducks.'

'I have—it's in my pocket,' said Katherine, and smiled at the doctor, who gave her a thoughtful look and didn't smile at all.

They ploughed through the snow, exchanging rather smug greetings with the few people they met, and caught brief snatches of, 'A splendid day to be outdoors,' and 'Have you seen the grotto?' or, even more frequently, 'They don't know what they are missing.'

Katherine, walking prudently in the doctor's size twelve footsteps in order to keep her feet as dry as possible, glowed with happiness; never mind tomorrow or the day after, she might not see him for days, even weeks, but just at the moment here he was within inches of her. She listened to Edward's voice, talking of this and that, and answered him light-heartedly and laughed a great deal. By the time they were half-way round the lake, with a brief stop at Diana's Temple, she was as warm as toast; the cold had put colour into her cheeks and her eyes sparkled so that she was almost pretty. The doctor, pausing from time to time, glanced at her, still with a thoughtful look which she didn't notice, and when they got to the winding stone steps leading to the grotto he handed the dogs to Edward. 'You go ahead. I'll give Katherine a hand, it may be slippery.'

As indeed it was. She slithered down with the doctor's hand firm under her elbow, as much agitated by his nearness as the icy steps. At the bottom he released her, and she went to look at Neptune and then the spring of almost freezing water. It was very cold, and the cobbled floor was slippery, but the view from the rough-hewn openings in the grotto's walls was well worth it. They came out into the open air again, and a watery, weak sun shone upon them. Ten minutes more and they would be back where they had started from. Katherine, who would have liked to have gone on walking for ever with the doctor, sighed gently.

'I've dropped a glove,' said Edward suddenly. 'I took it off to try the water in the grotto. I'll have to go back.'

'We'll go on—if you don't catch us up before, we'll be in the bar.'

The path was wide enough for them to walk side by side, Charlie and Flo trotting at their master's heels while he chatted pleasantly enough about Stourhead. 'Have you been to the house?' he wanted to know, and when she shook her head, 'I wouldn't care to live there myself, but the library is a splendid apartment, with some superb examples of Chippendale's work.'

He paused to look down at her eager face under the holly-berry-red cap. 'Will you marry me, Katie?'

His calm voice hadn't altered in the least.

Here she felt her heart give a great thud, stop for an amazed second and then begin to beat so fast that she caught her breath. 'Me?' she squeaked. 'Marry you?' She swallowed. 'Is it a joke or something?'

'Personally, I have never considered a proposal of marriage a joke.'

'Oh, I didn't mean that. I'm sorry, but I...you see, you're going to marry Dodie.'

She scanned his face, trying to read its expression. It told her nothing. 'Ah—you have heard that?'

'Well, yes—I mean everyone expects you to. Mr and Mrs Grainger, Tom Fetter—I heard him say one day that you had been waiting all these years for her to grow up so that you could marry her.'

'All these years.' His voice was quiet and without expression. 'Dodie is three years older than you are—twenty-four—I was twelve when she was born. More than a decade.'

She said worriedly, 'But being all that much older doesn't matter a bit. I mean, you don't seem to...that is, it's not even middle-aged.'

He smiled then. 'You reassure me, Katie.'

She said kindly, hiding her hurt, 'I expect you spoke without thinking—I often do. I'll forget it, I promise you. I expect you feel frustrated because Dodie isn't here.'

'So you think that I should marry Dodie as soon as possible?'

She nodded, unaware of the misery in her eyes. 'Oh, yes—she's very pretty.'

'That's a flimsy excuse for marriage. But I promise you I'll give it my earnest consideration.'

She was awash with misery. Here he was, the man she loved more deeply than anything on earth, and she was urging him to marry a girl who would make him unhappy for the rest of his life! She should have accepted him then and there, whatever the consequences. He didn't love her, of course; probably he had been imagining how she would react if he asked her to marry him and he had said it out loud, but she loved him enough for two, and she would be a good wife. Too late now and, even if she had known what to say, Edward was charging along the path towards them.

'Found it!' he bellowed. 'What a bit of luck. I say, I'm famished.'

They ate sausages and chips in the basket, and the men drank beer while Katherine had a pot of coffee and, at the doctor's instigation, a glass of brandy with it. It warmed her nicely, but there was an icy core deep inside her which she knew would only be melted by the doctor's love, and that wasn't going to happen, so she would have to learn to make the best of it.

'A pity the shop is closed, though I don't suppose it would do much business in this sort of weather.' Edward ate the last of his chips and sat back at his ease. 'I might have bought you a souvenir, Katherine.'

'I don't need a souvenir to remind me of such a super morning.'

'Very nicely put. You are no beauty, but you have charm.'

She laughed. 'I shall treasure that compliment.'

'Don't forget that you are coming to Jason's New Year's party.' He grinned. 'You don't need to look at him like that—the invitations are written, you'll get yours tomorrow. So trot out the best bib and tucker, do whatever it is women do to their faces, and present yourself at eight o'clock sharp on Old Year's Night.'

'You will be fetched,' interpolated the doctor. 'There will be quite a few people you already know— from the medical block, Matron, some of the sisters and the consultant and house surgeons from your side.'

'Oh, but I don't know them. At least, it's the other way round, they don't know me. I don't think they know I'm there.'

He smiled a little, remembering his colleague's reference to a pale brown mouse who scuttled into the sluice room as soon as he arrived on the ward.

'All the more reason,' declared Edward cheerfully, 'for you to wear something a bit way out, and take everyone by surprise.'

'I'll do my best.'

Presently, they drove back to Salisbury through the early dusk, the dogs snoring at their feet. Katherine, who had hoped that the doctor might suggest that she sit in front beside him, was disappointed to find herself ushered in with Edward and the dogs. She sup-

posed that she would be dropped off at Mrs Potts'
house, and thought up several suitable thank-you
speeches. On no account must she outstay her welcome; even if the doctor invited her back for tea it
would be because he had nice manners. She could
make some excuse if he did.

But at least part of her problem was solved for her.
They stopped in Shaftesbury and had teacakes and tea
in a well-lit, warm café in the centre of the town, and
when the doctor asked her what she was doing with
the evening, she crossed her fingers behind her back
and said composedly that she was going to the cinema
with Miss Kendall, one of her fellow lodgers. That
young lady was still away, but it was a small fib and
did no one any harm. The doctor concealed a smile,
for she was lying so earnestly and making heavy
weather of it, too, but all he said was, 'Oh, a pleasant
end to your day.'

Which gave her an opportunity to thank him.

They both got out of the car at Mrs Potts'. Edward
after a brief hug and a cheery 'see you', got into the
front seat, while the doctor unlocked the door for her
and waited until she was indoors before closing it
behind her with a brief, 'Goodbye, Katherine.'

At Stourhead that afternoon he had called her Katie; no one had called her that since her father and
mother had died, and it had warmed her heart to hear
him say it, but it seemed she was to be Katherine
once more. Which, in the circumstances, was fair
enough.

She wasn't on duty until twelve o'clock the next

day and, since her invitation to the party had arrived
by the morning's post, it seemed a good idea to comb
the dress shops for something to wear. The sales were
on, and she had enough money, she hoped, to find
something suitable. But what *was* suitable? There was
a splendid selection, and none of them too highly
priced. A pink satin dress with a sequined bodice
would certainly draw all eyes, so would a slinky black
velvet, although, if Matron was to be there, she might
not approve of the bodice, or what there was of it.
Finally, she settled on a silver-grey taffeta with a
square neckline and elbow-length sleeves; it was a
pretty dress in a demure way, and plain enough to go
unremembered on future occasions—if there were to
be any. It was calf-length, and the skirt was gently
gathered into a waistband which showed off her slim
waist to perfection. Her shoes wouldn't do; she
searched in all the cheaper shops without success, and
then found exactly what she wanted, grey velvet court
shoes going cheap because the bead work on the toe
had become a little tarnished.

There was barely time to make a cup of tea and
gobble down a sandwich when she got back to her
room, but the morning had been a success, and she
hadn't spent quite all of her money.

She went on duty in excellent spirits, which was
just as well, for Sister was at her most martial and
Andy was in a bad temper because she had quarrelled
with her boyfriend. The patients were pernickety, too,
suffering from too much Christmas fare and reaction
after the excitement of the last few days. No one

asked her if she had enjoyed her Christmas, although Staff Nurse observed that she was glad to see her back after her day off.

She was tired when she got back to her room later that evening; she ate the supper Mrs Potts had saved for her, helped to tidy away the meal when she had finished, and then went up to bed. Even the sight of her new dress failed to lift her spirits, and the very idea of going to the doctor's party filled her with doubts.

They were still there as she dressed on Old Year's Night. Perhaps no one would come to fetch her; perhaps no one there would bother to speak to her; probably her dress was all wrong... She had no jewellery save a good gold locket on an old-fashioned chain which had belonged to her grandmother; she put it on, powdered her nose once more, patted her already neat head into even more neatness, picked up her coat and went downstairs to the kitchen.

At least her fellow lodgers and Mrs Potts admired the dress; she was putting on her coat when Mrs Potts went to answer the door and came back with Edward. He breezed in, planted a kiss on her cheek, shook everyone else by the hand, gave Mrs Potts a box of chocolates and urged Katherine to get a move on. 'Jason's up to his eyeballs in half of Salisbury—you ought to see some of the girls' outfits!' He tucked her into the car and got in beside her. 'What's under the coat?'

'A dress,' said Katherine calmly. 'And don't expect anything breathtaking, because it's not.'

'I'll let you know when I see it.'

They arrived at the house, lights streaming from its windows and cars parked half-way down the street. Edward bustled her inside. The door was opened by a solemn, middle-aged man who wished her a good evening, and observed sternly, 'You were quick, Mr Edward.'

'Like the light, Coker.' Edward touched her arm. 'Katherine, this is Coker, Jason's right arm. Been with him man and boy, haven't you, Coker? You've not seen him before because he's been in hospital.' He handed his coat to him. 'It hasn't been the same without you, although Mrs Spooner did her valiant best.'

'Thank you, Mr Edward. If the young lady will go upstairs and leave her coat?'

He led the way up the graceful curved staircase, and opened a door on the landing above. There were coats everywhere; she added hers to the pile of furs and velvets on the bed, cast a quick look at herself in the pier-glass and followed Coker downstairs again. Edward was waiting for her, and she was pleased to see that he approved of her dress.

'Clever girl! You'll stand out like a nun at a circus.' Upon which heartening speech he swept her into the drawing-room.

There were a great many people there; she would never have dared go in on her own. She caught his sleeve and said urgently, 'Don't leave me alone for a bit, will you, Edward?'

He patted her hand. 'Count on me. Jason's seen us.'

The doctor was making his way towards them, pausing here and there to exchange a word. When he reached them he said, 'Thanks, Edward, I'll take Katherine to meet a few people. There's a smashing blonde by the fireplace, waiting for someone to rescue her...'

'Give a yell if you want me.' Edward gave her a wide grin and edged his way towards the other end of the room.

'I do like that dress.' The doctor smiled down at her, his eyes twinkling.

'Thank you.' She wasn't sure why she added, 'I almost didn't come...'

'I thought you might have doubts, but there has to be a beginning—the first step, as it were.'

She stared at him. He was elegant in his dinner-jacket, his face pleasantly calm but, she thought, tired. 'Towards what?' she wanted to know.

'Why, love, marriage, children—a lifetime of happiness.'

'You really believe that?'

'Yes—do you not?'

She nodded gravely. 'Oh, yes, but sometimes it's best not to take the step.'

He smiled suddenly. 'Am I being warned off?' And before she could say anything, he went on, 'Come and meet one or two people I think you might like.'

People who, strangely enough, had known her parents and who in turn introduced her to other younger men and women. Presently she found herself quite at ease and enjoying herself. True, there was a sprinkling of guests who ignored her completely, and she quickly discovered that they were friends of Dodie's. That young lady, holding court in the centre of the room, joined the small circle of people Katherine was with and brought their casual talk to an abrupt halt.

'Hello, Katherine!' She smiled brilliantly at her. 'So you managed to save enough wages to get a dress. In the sales? What a bit of luck for you, but an evening out like this is well worth going without your dinner to pay for it...'

She slid away before anyone could speak, until one of the girls said loudly, 'She's been drinking too much—she always does. Katherine, your dress is charming, we've all been admiring it. Tell me, what is your uniform like? I'd love to work in a hospital, but I'd be no good at it—only as a kitchen maid, and I can't even cook.'

The talk turned to cooking and food, and the unpleasant little incident was papered over by her companions' good manners. Katherine was glad that she had been too surprised to utter a word; to have made a scene at Jason's party would have been unforgivable, but perhaps that was what Dodie had hoped for. Edward took her to supper presently, a cold buffet laid out in the dining-room, presided over by Mrs Spooner and Coker and two girls wearing black dresses and white aprons. Edward nodded towards them. 'Sheila and Daphne—they help Mrs Spooner in the house—come each day.' He waved his fork at them and they smiled broadly at him.

'When do you go back to London?' asked Katherine, popping a tasty morsel of something cheesy into her mouth.

'Ah! In despair at the thought of me leaving you? In a couple of days, my dear. Jason's going to drive me up in the evening and stay for a short while—he hasn't had a break for months. I suppose Dodie will come with us, though it hasn't been mentioned. Have you seen her? I mean, to speak to?'

'Well, she spoke to me, but she'd gone again before I had a chance to say anything.'

Something in her voice made him look at her. 'Like that, was it? I shall miss you—I should have liked a sister like you...'

'Oh, Edward, what a nice thing to say! Thank you. I already have one brother, did you know?'

He nodded, and she went on: 'But he's a good deal older than I am—and he's rather serious. I'll gladly be a sister to you, Edward.'

'Exactly what I would wish to hear,' said the doctor's voice behind her. 'Are you enjoying yourself, Katherine? When are you on duty tomorrow?'

'At twelve o'clock.'

'Good. Wait behind until everyone has gone, and I'll take you back.'

'Oh, but I could...'

'Don't argue, Katherine.' He smiled briefly, and went to join some of his guests at another table.

There was champagne at midnight to celebrate the New Year, and within the hour the guests left. The last of them had been seen on their way by one o'clock, all save Dodie and a good-looking man in his thirties. His eyes were too close together, Katherine decided, and his dress too flamboyant. He lolled back in a chair while Dodie talked to the doctor. Katherine wasn't near enough to hear what she was saying, but the doctor's reply annoyed her, for she hunched her shoulders and turned away from him and ran across the room to throw her arms round the other man's neck.

'Well, if you won't take me, Nigel will.'

The doctor's voice was placid. 'My dear Dodie, I have a clinic in the morning at half-past eight—by all means let Nigel take you, if he will.'

'You cross old darling,' declared Dodie and shot a quick look at Katherine. 'Take me out to dinner in the evening and I'll let you announce our engagement.'

The doctor laughed. 'I'll take you out to dinner, but I'll not promise more than that.' He nodded at Nigel. 'Enjoy yourselves—Dodie, I'll give you a ring some time during the day.'

After they had gone, Coker appeared with a tray of coffee. 'I know you need to go to bed,' said the doctor, 'but this will warm you, and I promise you I'll have you back at Mrs Potts' within twenty minutes.'

Which he did, rather to Katherine's regret; a short night of sleeping was a small price to pay for his company. As he opened Mrs Potts' door and held it for her to go in, she paused to thank him. 'It was a lovely party,' she assured him, 'I met several people who knew my parents. It was like it used to be...'

'Will you marry me, Katie?'

She was so taken by surprise that she stammered a little. 'No—no, of course not!' She added, with something of a snap, 'You're taking Dodie out to dinner...'

'Ah, yes, but one must keep one's hand in!' He bent and kissed her swiftly. 'Goodnight, Katie.'

He pushed her into the narrow hall and closed the door, leaving her standing there, a prey to a variety of feelings, which were so strong that she cried while she undressed and got into bed. Tears were still trickling down her cheeks as, from sheer weariness, she slept at last.

Morning came much too soon; she got her breakfast, washed her smalls and, because Mrs Potts said she didn't feel very well, did her shopping for her before going on duty. Almost everyone on the ward was in a bad temper, due to not enough sleep on the previous night. Sister, castigating her for spilling water on the ward floor, gave it as her opinion that Katherine would never make a nurse, even if she ever applied to train as one.

'But I don't intend to,' objected Katherine politely, to be told sharply not to answer back.

'And what were you doing at Dr Fitzroy's party?' finished Sister darkly.

'I know his cousin, Edward,' said Katherine in a matter-of-fact voice.

Sister could do nothing more than utter, 'Oh, really?' Obviously, she hadn't expected such a simple explanation.

Mrs Potts looked ill when Katherine got back from the hospital. 'I've caught a cold,' she explained, 'and what can you expect in this weather? I'll be all right in the morning.'

Katherine left just before eight o'clock in the morning; it was one of her long days of duty, and she saw no one as she left the house. Mrs Potts, she suspected, was still in bed, nursing her cold.

The ward was busy, for it was take-in week again. Katherine trotted to and fro about her mundane tasks, thinking about Jason, wondering if he had enjoyed his evening with Dodie, and whether she had coaxed him at last into asking her to marry him. Katherine was very afraid that she might. He was far too good for her and inclined to laugh tolerantly at her tantrums. Perhaps they had known each other for such a long time that he no longer noticed them. But would Dodie make him happy? Tantrums in a pretty girl one took out to dinner and allowed the freedom of your home might not be so amusing in a wife. She frowned so heavily at the thought that the patient whose water jug she was filling asked her if she felt ill.

She was a little late going off duty, and the house, when she reached it, seemed very quiet. No one home, she decided, and stood in the hall, reading a hand-delivered letter from Edward on the eve of going back to London and, according to him, reluctant to go. He bade her a regretful goodbye, with the promise that he would be down to see her again as soon as he could get a weekend. 'Jason always puts me up,' he had told her. 'My people live in Cumbria, too far for a few days' leave.' She would miss him once he had gone back up to London, and it was nice of him to write. He missed her already, he wrote, and went on at some length to describe the nurse who had taken his fancy. Katherine laughed as she went up-stairs, eager to get to her room and make a pot of tea.

She was on the first landing when she heard a noise which made her pause. A small wheezing sound, and then a dry, difficult cough. It was coming from Mrs Potts' room. Katherine was aware that her landlady didn't encourage any intrusion into her private life; she looked after her lodgers very well, presided over her table in a friendly fashion, but no one, according to Miss Kendall, had ever been invited to have a chat in her room. Miss Kendall was still away, but surely Mrs Dunster or Miss Fish had noticed that their land-lady wasn't in the kitchen or sitting-room downstairs? There was no point in hesitating. Katherine knocked and went in.

It was dark already, but the curtains hadn't been drawn and there was no light. She advanced a few steps into the room and said softly, 'Mrs Potts? I'm sorry to intrude. I heard you coughing and I wondered if you were ill? Perhaps there is something I can do? A hot drink?'

Mrs Potts' voice—a croak, unlike her usual, brisk tones—came from the bed. 'The lamp on the table—by my bed.'

Katherine went cautiously forward to where the darker outline of a bed was visible. She found the lamp, switched it on and looked at Mrs Potts, lying there with a flushed face, wheezing and coughing her little dry cough.

'I feel ill,' she whispered unnecessarily.

Katherine felt for her pulse and put a hand on her hot forehead. 'Has anyone been in to see you? Have you had a drink?'

'No, love. Mrs Dunster and Miss Fish went downstairs a while ago, but I don't think they heard me call. They came back up to their rooms.'

'Look, if you don't mind, I'll get your doctor—I think you may have 'flu. But first I'll shake up your pillows and get you a drink.'

She sat Mrs Potts up and found another pillow, wiped her face with a wet cloth and combed back her hair, and then hurried down to the kitchen.

While the kettle boiled, she found a bottle of orange squash and made a jugful, then made tea and carried the tray upstairs. 'Drink this first,' she advised, proffering the cold drink. 'I'm going to telephone the doctor and then I'll come back and pour your tea. I'll leave the door open.'

Half-way to the door she paused. 'Who is your doctor, Mrs Potts?'

'Why, Dr Fitzroy, my dear.'

She had to look up his number, and it was Coker who answered. She explained in her quiet voice, and added, 'I think Mrs Potts is quite ill.'

'I'll fetch the doctor, miss,' said Coker, and a moment later Jason's voice, unhurried and calm, sounded in her ear.

He listened while she gave him the few details she had. 'I'll be round in about five minutes.' He rang off and she went back upstairs, meeting Miss Fish on the way.

'Why is no one in the kitchen getting our supper?' She gave Katherine an accusing stare.

'Mrs Potts isn't well—she's in bed. She's been there all day. Didn't you notice she wasn't around the house, Miss Fish?'

'It isn't my business to wonder about my land-lady's absence.'

'Well, I'm afraid you'll have to get your own suppers this evening.'

Katherine turned and ran downstairs again as the doorbell rang.

Dr Fitzroy came in, dwarfing his surroundings, ex-uding confidence and a soothing calm. 'In her room?' he asked and went upstairs, wishing Miss Fish a civil good evening as he passed her.

He took off his car coat and gave it to Katherine, and walked over to the bed. Mrs Potts peered up at him, coughed and said in a wheezy voice, 'I'm sorry to bother you, Doctor—it's only a cold, but I do feel poorly.'

He sat down beside the bed, took her pulse and asked a few questions in his calm way. And then he said, 'If Katherine will help you, I should like to ex-amine your chest, Mrs Potts.'

He got up and walked to the window when he had finished, and stood looking out into the street below until Katherine had Mrs Potts tidily arranged against her pillows once more. 'I should like you to come into hospital for a few days, Mrs Potts. You have 'flu and a touch of pneumonia. We can have you back on your feet again in no time at all with antibiotics, but you will have to stay in bed and be nursed, so that's the best place for you.'

'Who is to look after the house and my lodgers?' whispered Mrs Potts. 'I can't leave them…'

'I shall ask Mrs Spooner to come and stay—we can manage without her for a few days. Now, Katherine will wrap you up warm, and I'll take you back with me and then fetch Mrs Spooner…'

'They'll be wanting their supper…'

'I'll see to that, Mrs Potts,' said Katherine, her head in the wardrobe, looking for woollies and a dressing-gown, 'and I'm not on duty until noon tomorrow, so I can cast an eye over the house in the morning.'

It took time and patience to get Mrs Potts swathed in a variety of woollies and blankets; the doctor carried her downstairs and Katherine went ahead to open the door and then the car door. 'Can you manage?' she wanted to know. 'Shall I telephone the hospital and let them know you're coming?'

He had the car phone in his hand. 'I'll do that now. Get inside before you catch your death of cold. I'll bring Mrs Spooner along as soon as I can.'

'No need to hurry. I'll get supper and make up Mrs Potts' bed ready for her.' She poked her head into the back of the car. 'I'll come and see you tomorrow. Be good, Mrs Potts, and don't worry about a thing—just get well.'

'Miss Fish, Mrs Dun—' began Mrs Potts.

'I'll keep an eye on them.' She bent and kissed Mrs

Potts' hot forehead, because she looked so ill and for-lorn, and then closed the door and found the doctor right behind her. He said impatiently, 'I said, go in-doors.'

She went without a backward glance, feeling put out. He could have said thank you, instead he had sounded annoyed. Perhaps he had planned to spend the evening with Dodie.

She went straight to the kitchen and opened a can of soup, inspected the fridge and decided on omelettes and tinned peas, and the remains of a treacle tart. While she was laying the table, her fellow lodgers joined her.

'Supper is late,' complained Mrs Dunster, and sat down at the table, presumably expecting it to be set before her.

Katherine explained, and was met by a disapprov-ing sniff. 'How very inconvenient,' observed Mrs Dunster. When Miss Fish joined her, she relayed the news with a few embellishments of her own. The two ladies grumbled genteelly together while Katherine got their supper and, having eaten it, rose from the table and went up to their rooms, leaving the remains of their meal for her to clear away. But first she would have to get a room ready for Mrs Spooner. Finding clean bedlinen took a few minutes, but she had be-come quite expert at making up beds since she had been at the hospital. She had the room to rights in no time at all, and sped to her room to hang up her things. It was icy-cold there, and she was tempted to light the gas fire, but there was still the best part of an hour's work in the kitchen. She nipped downstairs once more and contemplated the mess there.

The front door bell went just as she had tied herself into one of Mrs Potts' aprons; it was Mrs Spooner, with the doctor looming behind her.

Katherine bade them come in, and Mrs Spooner gave her a worried smile. 'Poor Emily,' she said, 'alone all day. Well, as good as alone, with those two old women not even noticing that she wasn't there.'

She sniffed, and Katherine made haste to say, 'Well, I think they spend a lot of time in their rooms, but it must have been most unpleasant for Mrs Potts.'

They had all gone into the kitchen, and Mrs Spooner eyed the mess in a severe way, so that Katherine felt constrained to tell her that she had been on the point of washing up and tidying everything away. 'But we've had supper,' she added quickly. 'Not quite what Mrs Potts would have given us…'

'Bless you, miss, and you with a day's work behind you. I'll have Emily's room, shall I? I'll just make up the bed.'

'I've done that—that's why the kitchen's untidy.' Katherine sounded apologetic, and the doctor, standing silently, allowed a small sound to escape his lips.

'Perhaps if you'd like to go upstairs with Mrs Spooner, I might make a start on this?'

Both ladies looked at him with horror. Mrs Spooner's outraged 'sir' was a fraction ahead of Katherine's, 'You can't wash up, you don't know how!'

He was taking off his coat. 'I never could resist a challenge,' he told her blandly. 'Off you go and count the sheets or whatever you need to do, and we'll have a pot of tea when you come down.'

In Mrs Potts' bedroom, her sister sat down on the basket-work chair by the window, and Katherine perched on the bed. Mrs Spooner had everything nicely planned; for the greater part of the day she would be there, and when Katherine got back from work perhaps she wouldn't mind keeping an eye on things while she went back to the doctor's house and made sure that Coker and the girls were managing. Her tone implied that they would make a mess of things without her. 'And then I could pop in and see Emily on the way back.'

Katherine explained her off-duty hours. 'And of course I'll do all I can to help. I hope it won't be for too long. It must be awkward for you.'

'She'd do the same for me,' observed Mrs Spooner, 'and I must say you are very kind, miss. We'd better go down and see how the doctor's getting on.'

He was getting on very nicely; in his shirtsleeves now, with a pipe in his mouth. Miss Fish and Mrs Dunster would smell smoke in the morning and complain, but that didn't matter.

Mrs Spooner took the tea towel from him and said firmly, 'Now, sir, sit down, do. We've got everything nicely fixed up, and you must be wanting to go home...'

'Not before a cup of tea.'

They drank it sitting round the kitchen table, and presently he got up and put on his jacket and coat, then went to the door. 'Come and lock up behind me,

Katherine.' His voice was mild enough, but she found herself following him into the hall.

They stood together, of necessity rather squashed in the narrow space. 'Not quite the evening I had planned, but most satisfactory.' He opened the door with one hand, and caught her close with his other arm and kissed her hard. 'Thank you, Katie. Our paths cross so often, they are bound to converge one day.'

CHAPTER EIGHT

KATHERINE floated back into the kitchen on a cloud of enchanted rapture, to come back to earth with a terrific thump when Mrs Spooner observed, 'He'll be late for their evening out, and Miss Dodie does hate to be kept waiting—she'll have gone off in a huff, more like.' Mrs Spooner's sniff expressed her opinion better than any words. 'Never one to shirk his duty is the doctor—loves his work and hasn't much time for parties and so on—of course, he's a lot older than Miss Dodie—I dare say she'll settle down once she's married.' She glanced at Katherine. 'You look tired, miss—you go off to bed or you won't be fit for work tomorrow. On in the afternoon, the doctor said.'

'Yes, that's right, Mrs Spooner. Would you like to go and see Mrs Potts before lunch? I don't leave here until just before noon. I could do any shopping you want when I go out in the morning—you'd have time to go to the doctor's house, too.'

'Well, that's a nice idea—you wouldn't mind?'

'Not a bit, only I do have to go before lunch, but I expect you've got a key? If you would make a list of shopping, I'll leave it on the table here.'

'That would suit me. And since you're being so kind you'll take your breakfast here—that way you'll get a bit of a lie-in.'

'Oh, but won't that be extra work for you?'

'Bless you, no, miss. You come down around eight o'clock and I'll have it ready for you.' She nodded in a satisfied way. 'It's a good thing that the doctor and Mr Edward are going up to London tomorrow evening—they'll go to the doctor's flat. He won't be back for a day or two. All the same, I'd like to pop in each day...'

'Yes, of course. You'll let me know if there is anything I can do to help?'

She wished Mrs Spooner goodnight, and went to her room to make a pot of tea and allow common sense to take over from the romantic dreams of her heart. The doctor had meant nothing by his kiss, and his remark about their paths made no sense at all. She got into bed and lay thinking about it and presently went to sleep—for, however deeply in love she might be, she was dog-tired.

A week went busily by; the ward was still full, and winter colds and 'flu were taking their toll of staff. Besides, there was Mrs Spooner to give a helping hand to, and Mrs Potts to visit each day—something Katherine looked forward to in the hope that she would see Jason. He was away for two days but he still did his usual mid-week round because Andy, who knew everyone and got all the news, had told her so. But Katherine never managed to be on the ward when he was there, nor did she see him around the hospital, despite the fact that she took long and devious ways in which to come and go. On her days off, too, she was unlucky, and on the last day of the week Mrs Potts was to return home.

Mrs Spooner and Katherine, making up the bed ready for her and putting flowers in a vase, discussed the next week or two's plans. Mrs Spooner was to return to the doctor's house that evening and one of the young women who came each day to help in his house would come to Mrs Potts instead. And, as soon as she was well enough, she was to have a short holiday. 'The doctor has a cottage at Bucklers Hard, a nice, quiet place at this time of year, and as cosy a little house as you could wish for. Just the thing for a few days' rest,' explained Mrs Spooner.

Katherine agreed, wishing for an impossible miracle which would make it possible for her to go there too, as Mrs Potts' companion. On the other hand, it would mean that she would have no chance of seeing the doctor at all, whereas now, each day brought the possibility of seeing him.

She was on duty when Mrs Potts returned, to be told on her return that Dr Fitzroy had driven her back himself with one of his daily maids; he had stayed and had a cup of tea, Shirley Kendall told her when she got back from the hospital, and then gone up to Mrs Potts' room to make sure that she was all right.

'I could go for him in a big way,' declared Shirley. 'Ever so polite, he is; makes you feel you're important, if you know what I mean.' She gave Katherine an envious glance. 'I expect you see a lot of him at the hospital.'

'Almost never. I'm on the surgical side and Dr

Fitzroy's a consultant on the medical wards. Consultants don't hobnob with nursing auxiliaries.'

'Bit of a snob, is he?'

'Heavens, no! We just don't meet. Did you have a nice holiday?'

'You bet—there was this man…' Shirley embarked on a long and involved account of someone's cousin who had turned up unexpectedly. 'He's coming to take me out next weekend…he's got a Ford Escort…'

Katherine was to have days off on the following weekend. She had put in a good deal of overtime since Christmas, filling gaps where the staff had been ill and, very much to her surprise, Sister had told her that she might have what amounted to a long weekend: Friday from one o'clock until Monday noon.

Katherine spent the week trying to decide what to do with this unexpected treat; she had a little money by now, and she might employ Saturday browsing round the sales, for her wardrobe was still woefully scanty. She might have a meal out and perhaps go to the theatre. It was a pity that Shirley had a date with the man she had met at Christmas, and that Andy would be on duty over the weekend. She would certainly go to the library and get something to read, and there was the cathedral on Sunday—she occupied herself in filling her days; weekends didn't often come her way.

It was on Friday morning that she received a summons to go to Sister's office; she had been making beds with one of the student nurses, now she muttered an apology and hurried down the ward—one didn't keep Sister waiting—wondering what she had done wrong. Or perhaps her weekend off had been quashed...

Sister was looking severe, sitting with a poker-straight back behind her desk, and lounging against the radiator was Dr Fitzroy.

He stood up as Katherine went in, and Sister said, 'Katherine, Dr Fitzroy has a favour to ask of you.'

Miracles weren't always impossible, she thought bemusedly, listening to him suggesting in a cool, impersonal manner that he would be vastly obliged if she would accompany Mrs Potts down to Bucklers Hard. 'Just to see her safely in. Someone will go down on Monday morning to stay with her, but it would oblige me if you could see your way to staying until then. I understand that it is your weekend off, but perhaps you have other plans?'

'No, I haven't,' said Katherine joyfully, and beamed at him. 'I'll be glad to go.'

He studied her thoughtfully. 'Yes, good. You and Mrs Potts will be fetched from her house after lunch today, and transport will be arranged for your return on Monday morning. Thank you, Katherine.'

It was cool dismissal. She said 'Thank you, sir' and looked at Sister. 'You may go, Katherine.' She was dismissed again, and got herself out of the office, not looking at the doctor at all, and went back to making beds. It was lovely to have her weekend so splendidly filled, but need he have been quite so remote in his manner? It was no good worrying about it; she fell to deciding what to wear...

The snow had turned to rain and there was a cold wind with it; she got away from the hospital punctually, and hurried back to her room, ate a quick meal of beans on toast and the inevitable pot of tea, and packed her night things. She got into the wool dress once more, and went to see how Mrs Potts was faring. She was dressed, ready to go, and Katherine helped her downstairs to sit in the kitchen, in the warm, while she fetched their cases. They didn't have to wait long; Katherine went to open the door when the bell rang, and found the doctor on the doorstep.

His eyes swept over her neat person. 'Ready? And Mrs Potts?'

When she nodded, he went into the kitchen and led Mrs Potts out to the car, stowing her into the back seat with the two dogs. The cases he put in the boot, then he urged Katherine to get in beside him and drove off without further ado.

He took the main road out of the city, but at Downton he turned off towards Cadnam and once there took the main road again to Brockenhurst. He had little to say as he drove and Katherine, happy just to be beside him, kept quiet. They were through Brockenhurst on the way to Beaulieu and Bucklers Hard before he remarked, 'You'll doubtless find the cottage well-stocked with food. There's central heating, and fires, and someone will have been in to keep it tidy and make up the beds and so on. I don't expect you to be with Mrs Potts every minute of the day—take time off for a walk—you look as though you could do with some fresh sea air. There's a nice little pub close by, and the cottage is the end one in a row, so you don't need to be lonely. Don't let Mrs Potts go out in this weather, but I'd like her to potter around the house a bit. By the end of the week she should be pretty fit.'

She said meekly, 'Yes, sir,' and gave a surprised start when he growled, 'Don't call me sir, Katie.' Then, in a quite different voice, he asked, 'Have you given any more thought to marrying me?'

She had to admit silently that one way or another she had thought of exceedingly little else, but all she said, in a collected voice, was, 'I do wonder why you keep on about it.'

'Ah, that is at least a step in the right direction. What a pity that we have no more time in which to discuss the matter thoroughly.'

He had turned into the broad roadway leading to the quay and Beaulieu river. There were cottages on either side of it, and a hotel at the very end. He stopped at the last cottage on the opposite side and said, 'Stay there a moment while I open up,' and got out of the car to cross the narrow strip of grass and unlock the door. There was no garden at the front, but the cottage was solidly built of red brick, its paint-work fresh and its small windows gleaming. Even in the dull light of a January afternoon it looked inviting. Katherine jumped out when he opened her door, possessed herself of Mrs Potts' various scarves, rugs and handbag, and followed the doctor and her landlady into the cottage.

The doctor switched on a light once they were inside, revealing a small, square hallway with a door on either side and a staircase facing them. The doctor opened a door and ushered them into a low-ceilinged room with windows at either end. There was a bright fire burning in the small grate, and the furniture was exactly right: comfortable chairs and small, antique pieces arranged on a dark red carpet, matching the red and cream chintz curtains. 'I'll get your cases,' he said. 'We might have tea before I go back; the kitchen is through the door.' He nodded towards a small door at the far end of the room, and Katherine, taking the hint for the wish, sat Mrs Potts down and went to investigate. There was a tray already set for tea, with a large cake beside it and a dish of scones as well. There was cream too, and a pot of jam, so it only remained to put the kettle on. She went back to Mrs Potts, helped that lady to remove her coat and wraps, and then fetched the tray and set it on the round table in one corner of the room. She just had time to take off her own outdoor things before the doctor, with the dogs at his heels, came back with their cases. He went straight upstairs with them, which gave her time to light the gas under the kettle and find a bowl for the dogs to have a drink. He tossed his coat on to a chair and followed her into the kitchen.

'There's no back door,' he told her. 'I'll make sure that the heating is OK before I go. There should be plenty of hot water, and the bedrooms are warm. If you get into any difficulties, go across to the hotel and ask for the landlord.'

He watched her warm the pot and then spoon in the tea. 'You look just right here—I thought you would.' Before she could think of an answer to that, he had gone back into the sitting-room, and when she went in he was sitting by Mrs Potts, giving her last-minute instructions as to what she might and might not do.

Tea was a pleasant meal; the doctor showed no signs of hurry on his part, and it was well past five o'clock when he got up to go. Katherine went with him to the door, reluctant to see the last of him.

'It's getting dark, so drive carefully,' she cautioned him.

'You sound exactly like a wife,' he observed, 'so I feel quite justified in behaving like a husband.' He swooped down, scooped her into his arms and kissed her once, very hard. 'I'll see you on Monday morning.'

He got into the car and drove off. Although she was in the doorway watching, he didn't look round or wave. She went back indoors and cleared away the tea things, and then she accompanied Mrs Potts upstairs.

There were three bedrooms, two in the front of the house, which she and Mrs Potts were to occupy and a third beside a splendidly fitted bathroom across the landing. Katherine unpacked for them both, turned down the beds and drew the curtains and, with Mrs Potts in tow, went downstairs again.

Mrs Potts was tired, and Katherine suggested an early supper. 'You sit down for a while and I'll see what there is in the fridge,' she suggested, and went back into the kitchen.

Someone had catered very nicely for their needs; there was a casserole to be warmed up, potatoes already peeled and fruit and custard in a bowl. Katherine found a cloth and cutlery, and arranged the table; while the food cooked, she went to look at the room on the other side of the hall. The dining-room—with a mahogany table at its centre, with four chairs and a small side table. There was a long case clock in one corner, and some charming watercolours on the striped wallpaper. It really was a dear little house, she decided; just the place to come for a quiet weekend. And in the summer one could sail...

'Does the doctor come here often?' she asked.

'Quite a bit, my sister says; likes to get away when he's been busy at the hospital—he's got a boat too. Likes to sail for as much of the year as possible. Of course, Miss Dodie can't bear it here, says it's too quiet for her. Thinks she can twist him round her little finger, but she's wrong there.' She cast a quick look at Katherine. 'He's a good man, too good for her, though I say it as shouldn't.'

Katherine agreed quietly; he was a good man and a splendid doctor—also, he knew how to kiss a girl! Still glowing from it, she reflected that on no account must he do it again, it was too unsettling. Even if she hadn't been in love with him, it would have shaken her; as it was, she wasn't sure if she was on her head or her heels!

There was no point in dwelling upon that; she set-

tled Mrs Potts by the fire with a glass of the port the
doctor had said she must have each evening, and went
to the kitchen to cast an eye over the casserole.

They went to bed really early, for Mrs Potts was
tired out and, although there was television to watch,
Katherine felt lonely sitting by herself. Saturday
passed quietly, and Katherine didn't like to leave Mrs
Potts alone. But by Sunday, she had regained some
of her energy. The rain had ceased in the morning,
and the wind had died down. Katherine tidied the little cottage, took Mrs Potts her breakfast in bed and,
later, once she had helped her downstairs to sit by the
fire, she got into her coat and headscarf and went for
a brisk walk before lunch.

The fridge was still well stocked; she popped a
small chicken into the oven, peeled potatoes and
cleaned sprouts, and then went to keep Mrs Potts
company.

'Ever so awkward, it's been,' averred Mrs Potts,
'me being ill like this. And everyone's been so kind,
I'm that grateful.' She sounded almost tearful, so
Katherine was constrained to nip across the street and
buy a Sunday paper. They shared it between them
while the chicken roasted, and presently, when they
had eaten it, she tucked Mrs Potts up in her bed for
a nap and went to sit by the fire and dream. A useless
occupation, she reminded herself as the afternoon
dimmed into a rainy evening, and she washed up the
dinner things, then made tea and went to fetch a much
refreshed Mrs Potts.

They watched television in the evening, and after

supper Mrs Potts went to bed. 'A whole week of this,' she commented blissfully. 'I feel better already. I'm ever so grateful to you, my dear, putting yourself out like this.'

'I've not been put out at all,' protested Katherine, 'I'm enjoying it just as much as you are. This is a super little cottage.' She tucked Mrs Potts into her bed. 'I'll bring you a cup of tea in the morning, but if you need anything in the night, just give me a call.'

The rain had stopped in the morning, leaving a pale, washed-out sky, and sunshine which held no warmth, although it turned the river and the fields into delicate pastel tints. It was cold, too. Katherine cleared away the ashes in the sitting-room, lit another fire, tidied the cottage, and, since she didn't know exactly when she was to be fetched, put a coffee tray ready. She made sure that Mrs Potts was cosily settled by the hearth, and then went briskly down to the river for a last look. She didn't stay long, there was still lunch to prepare for whoever was coming to take her place. The lunch was well in hand when the cottage door opened and the doctor came in, followed by Daphne—whom Katherine had first met at his house, helping with the supper, on New Year's Eve.

If Katherine had been hoping for a leisurely hour drinking coffee and chatting with him, she was disappointed; he drank his coffee, certainly, but beyond examining Mrs Potts and declaring that she was looking better already, and asking in a brisk manner if there were any problems with the running of the cottage, he had almost nothing to say beyond begging

Katherine to be as quick as possible since he had an appointment at noon.

A remark which sent her, with a scalded tongue from the coffee, running upstairs to get her case. When she got downstairs again, rather pink in the face, he observed belatedly, 'I'm sorry to hurry you, Katherine.'

She eyed him coldly. 'Think nothing of it Dr Fitzroy. Hurrying from here to there is becoming second nature to me.' And, at his raised eyebrows, 'On the ward, you know.'

In the car, going smoothly along the narrow road to Beaulieu, the doctor said with deceptive blandness, 'You're annoyed?'

'Annoyed? Me?' She ignored her companion's gentle correction to 'I'. 'Why should I be?'

'I'm treating you like a hired help...?' the doctor said, as they picked up speed, for the road had widened once they had passed the park gates.

'But I *am* a hired help,' Katherine pointed out. Usually a mild-tempered and reasonable girl, she felt decidedly snappy.

'But not quite in the mood to consider a proposal of marriage?'

'Certainly not.' She wasn't sure whether to burst out laughing or crying.

'Ah, well, another time.' He sounded positively placid.

'I'm getting tired...' began Katherine crossly.

'Indeed? And so am I, but tiredness was never a good reason for giving up, you know.'

He was deliberately misunderstanding her; she stared out at the busy main street of Brockenhurst and said nothing.

When he spoke again, it was to comment lightly about the weather—the chance of more snow, the prospect of an early spring. She answered him at random, only half listening, her thoughts in a fine muddle.

He left her at Mrs Potts' front door and drove off at once with the briefest of goodbyes. She went to her room to eat a hasty snack lunch before going to the hospital.

It was nice to find that Sister had a day off, and that Andy was on duty, too. Katherine was immediately immersed in her mundane duties, which, without Sister breathing down her neck, she found pleasant enough. The patients, aware that there was a certain relaxed air on the ward, called across to each other's beds and joked with the nurses, offering sweets and, when it was time to go off duty, proffering their newspapers.

Katherine, back at Mrs Potts', ate the supper waiting for her and repaired to her room to undress, scamper down to the bathroom and then get into bed with a mug of tea and the selection of papers thrust upon her when she had left the ward. She read them from cover to cover, not taking in a word, while she speculated as to what the doctor might be doing. Being very much in love, and having a lively imagination, she pictured him in some softly lit restaurant, dining with Dodie. Or perhaps the girl was at his house, sitting by his fireside, looking prettier than ever in the firelight.

She was not to know that he was still in the hospital, using all his skill to keep alive a young man who had had a massive coronary.

He certainly wasn't thinking of Dodie, nor for that matter of Katherine. Only when he got home at last, and he had eaten the solitary meal waiting for him, did he sit down beside his fire, the dogs at his feet, and allow his thoughts to wander. And they were all of Katherine.

Katherine didn't see him for some days, and then only at a distance, going in or out of the hospital or on the stairs or going along a corridor. And each time she took good care to avoid coming face to face with him.

She had been working when he had brought Mrs Potts back, and she returned one evening to find that lady installed in her kitchen once more, almost as good as new, and anxious to take up the reins of the household again. The talk, naturally enough, was of her week at Bucklers Hard, the comfort of the cottage and the kindness of the doctor, and she constantly referred to Katherine for confirmation of this. 'Kindness itself, wasn't he, Katherine? Driving us there and then fetching you back again, and then coming for me himself, and him such a busy man.'

To all of which Katherine agreed in her quiet voice; he was everything Mrs Potts declared him to be, and he was as distant from her as the stars.

She was on duty at twelve o'clock the following

day, and she was met by an intrigued Andy. 'I say,' she began the moment Katherine was on the ward, 'what luck Sister's off duty! You've had a phone call—can you beat it? He was very disappointed that he couldn't speak to you, but he gave me a message. Would you meet him at Snell's for coffee in the morning at half-past ten? He asked when you were off duty, and so I told him. Hope that was OK?'

Edward, back for a few days' leave, thought Katherine; he had promised to let her know when he was back in Salisbury. 'Thanks, Andy, but I must tell him not to phone the ward. What a blessing Sister wasn't here!'

They giggled about it together as they made beds ready for the evening and then went to collect the tea trays. It would be nice to see him again, reflected Katherine. He was good-natured and cheerful and easy-going.

She got to Snell's punctually, her shopping basket over her arm, having prudently done her errands on the way to the café; Edward was a great talker, and she would have to hurry back to get her lunch before going on duty.

Snell's was full, she stood in the doorway, scanning the tables, and presently saw her caller, only it wasn't Edward, whom she'd expected to see, it was her brother, standing up and beckoning her to join him.

She calmed her breath and sat down opposite him. 'Did you telephone the hospital?' she asked. There was no point in greeting him, for he showed no sign of pleasure at seeing her.

'I did. And if you want to know how I discovered where you were hiding, Mrs Todd saw you a couple of days ago when she visited her daughter.'

'I wasn't hiding...'

'Well, now we know where you are. You must come back, Katherine. Joyce isn't at all well, and the children are too much for her. The least you can do is show some gratitude and repay our kindness.'

She stared at him; he was, if that were possible, more pompous than ever, and his voice was louder and more hectoring.

She said quietly, 'Sorry, Henry, but I'm not coming back. I owe you nothing, and if Joyce isn't well you can afford to get proper help. I have a good job, I'm paid for it and I like my work.' She broke off as a waitress enquired if they would like coffee, and Henry gave a grudging order.

He goggled at her. 'Do you mean to say that you refuse to help your own flesh and blood?'

'That's right, Henry.' She sipped her coffee and he fell silent, bereft of words. 'Is that your last word?'

'Yes, Henry.' She sat composedly watching him and finishing her coffee.

He got up abruptly. 'Then there is no more to be said. Joyce will be bitterly disappointed...'

'So I should imagine.' She put out a hand and caught his coat by the sleeve. 'Henry, you are forgetting—the bill...'

His glare should have annihilated her, but quite failed to do so. He took the bill from the waitress and stalked off to pay it.

Reaction set in when he had gone; Katherine found herself shaking with rage. Her new-found freedom had been, for the moment at least, shattered. There was nothing more he could do, but it had left an unpleasant blot on her day. She had another cup of coffee and pulled herself together, then went back to her room to get her lunch.

It was very nearly time for her to go off duty that evening when she ran full-tilt into the doctor as she was on her way to the ward with some X-rays. She had expected that he would pass her with a brief nod, or even no greeting at all, but he stopped beside her.

'Katherine!' His voice was sharp. 'Why are you looking like that? What's worrying you?'

Naturally she said 'nothing', which was a waste of time, for he gave an impatient grunt and said, 'Don't waste time. I'm busy and so are you.'

She saw at once that she wasn't going to get away without answering him. 'My brother—he found out that I was here—I saw him this morning, he wants me to go back because Joyce isn't well. I said I wouldn't—and he was annoyed.'

His blue eyes studied her worried face. 'There's not much he can do then, is there? You're not afraid of him?'

She gave a surprised look. 'Heavens, no! But he upsets me.'

'A pity I have an engagement this evening. We might have discussed the matter.' He went on smoothly, watching her face. 'I have a date with Dodie.'

She had to say *something*, even if it was inane, 'Well, yes, I expect you have. I won't keep you, she hates to be kept waiting.'

'Yes, she does. Now, *I* could wait for ever for something or someone I wanted.' Without altering his voice in any way, he added, 'Is *this* the right moment for a proposal, Katie?'

She gave him a startled look and, quite bewildered by his serious face, flew away from him, not slowing her pace until she had put a corner of the corridor between them.

When her days off came, she spent them pottering around the shops, giving Mrs Potts a helping hand from time to time and walking in the cathedral grounds. She had managed to dispel the unwelcome meeting with Henry from her mind; Jason had said that there was nothing her brother could do, and she accepted that with relief. She did her best not to think about Jason, although she wasn't very successful. On the whole, she was glad to go back to work in the morning.

She had just finished bed-bathing a testy old gentleman with a badly injured arm and a nasty temper when Andy came bounding up the ward.

'Matron says you are to go to her office at once,' she breathed. 'Have you done something awful?'

Katherine eased her patient into his pyjama jacket and buttoned it up. 'Me? No.'

'Perhaps she's going to ask you if you would like to do your training?'

'Well, I wouldn't have thought so. Am I tidy?'

'Good enough. Your nose is shining, but Matron approves of that, anyway.'

Katherine made her way down to the office, knocked on the door and was bidden to enter.

Matron sat at her desk, severe, outsized authority, but with no sign of annoyance upon her regular features. 'Ah, Miss Marsh...' She paused at the look on Katherine's face as she saw Henry standing away from the desk, watching her. 'As you see, your brother is here to beg me to release you from your duties, so that you may return with him to look after his wife. I understand that she is gravely ill with anaemia.'

Clever Henry! He had her in a tight corner, but Katherine did her best.

'I think that my brother would do better to get a nurse to look after my sister-in-law. We don't get on very well, and a stranger is often more suitable. Or what about getting her into hospital if she is so ill?'

Matron looked shocked. 'There is, of course, that alternative, but I should have thought that a member of the family, very able to undertake nursing duties, would have been an ideal arrangement.' She paused and, since Katherine said nothing, added, 'Well, might it be a good idea if you were to go with your brother for a day or so and see how things are? If Mrs Marsh is seriously ill, I have no doubt she will be admitted as a patient, and you will be free to return to your duties here.'

'No, I won't,' Katherine said desperately. 'I shall

be expected to stay and look after the two children and run the house.'

Matron cast a glance at Henry, standing silent with a resigned look upon his face. Katherine looked at him, too; the two-faced villain!

'I can't force you,' he uttered in a sad voice, and he smiled wistfully.

'I really think that you should go, Miss Marsh. Change into your own clothes and go straight back with your brother. No doubt you can collect a few necessities later on from your lodgings. At least go and see if you are needed.'

Of course she would be needed, thought Katherine furiously. There would be the washing and the ironing and cooking and the children, as well as Joyce. Perhaps she really was ill, though. She would have to go, even if it was only for a day or so, while Henry made other arrangements.

She said, 'Very well, Matron,' and, to Henry, 'I'll be outside in ten minutes.'

'God bless you, my dear,' said Henry. He sounded thankful, but she could see the small, self-satisfied smirk on his face.

She went back to the ward, and found Andy in the sluice. 'I have to go back with my brother; he says his wife is very ill. I don't want to go, Andy, but I can't get out of it. If anyone wants to know where I am, will you tell them? And could you please phone Mrs Potts and tell her I'll be back as soon as I can. I'll explain later.'

She went to the office and reported to Sister, who

said crossly, 'I find it very annoying that my staff should be taken from me in this arbitrary manner. Kindly return as quickly as possible, Miss Marsh.'

Katherine got into her clothes, hung her uniform neatly in her locker and went the long way round to the entrance in the hope of seeing Jason. But she didn't see him, although he saw her, standing at a ward window looking out on to the forecourt. Now why, he reflected, should Katie be getting into a car and leaving the hospital when she was supposed to be on duty? He went back to his round, setting aside his thoughts of her until he had finished it, had coffee with the ward sister, given a multitude of instructions to his registrar and gone to the consultants' room, where he sat down and pondered about what he had seen. Presently, he went over to the telephone and rang Mrs Potts, and got scant satisfaction there. After a moment, he got up and went to the surgical block. On the men's ward, his polite request to have a few words with the nursing auxiliary known as Andy met with Sister's lifted eyebrows and a cold assent. He ignored both, and strolled down the ward to where Andy was taking round the dinner trays.

'A word with you, if you please.'

His quiet voice caused her to rattle the knives and forks in her hands. 'Me? You want to talk to me, sir?'

'Indeed I do. I hope you may be able to help me—er—Andy. Why has Katherine left the hospital?'

'She didn't say much, there wasn't time, but she asked me to tell anyone who asked that she had had to go to her brother because his wife was very ill. I suppose it would be to his house, but I don't know. She didn't want to go. Matron sent for her.'

Dr Fitzroy leaned his length against the end of an empty bed. 'Ah—you have been most helpful, Andy. I am indebted to you.'

He gave her a charming smile and left her with a head swarming with any number of exciting thoughts.

Dr Fitzroy went back to the consultants' room and picked up the telephone once more, dialled a number and, when someone answered, said, 'Dick, you have almost everyone along the Wylye Valley, haven't you? Would you check on one of your patients for me?'

He listened without interrupting, uttered his thanks and put down the receiver, glanced at his watch and sighed. He had two new patients to see on women's medical, and then an out-patient clinic starting at one o'clock. He stood thinking for a long minute, and then picked up the telephone and dialled once more. 'Mrs Spooner? Can you contrive a meal which can be dished up at any moment this evening? And I shall have a guest.'

He listened to his housekeeper patiently while she rearranged his dinner out loud. 'That sounds splendid, Mrs Spooner.' He rang off and made his way, placidly, unhurriedly, to the medical wing.

'What exactly is wrong with Joyce?' asked Katherine as Henry drove out of the hospital forecourt.

Henry chuckled. 'You heard what I described to Matron.'

'Yes. Is she in bed? And if she's so ill, why isn't she in hospital having treatment? And if she's at home, why haven't you got any help? You can afford it, Henry.'

He blustered a little. 'Why should I pay a woman to do the work you can do? You are my sister, you owe me something. Besides, Joyce is delicate.'

'What?' Katherine was trying to keep calm, and finding it very difficult. 'Joyce—delicate? What utter rubbish, Henry! She's always been lazy, and so have you.' She heard Henry gobbling with rage beside her, but her new-found independence had given her the courage to voice her opinion. 'It seems that I have no option but to come with you, but I warn you that I don't intend to stay. If Joyce is as ill as you made her out to be, then the best thing you can do is to get her to hospital and get some help in the house. And if she isn't ill, then I shall go straight back to work.'

He said sulkily, 'Well, you can find out for your-self.'

A remark which left her in sudden doubt; perhaps Joyce was really ill, in which case common humanity would force her to stay. Her spirits sank as they stopped outside the gate.

Joyce was in the sitting-room, standing before the nice mirror over the fireplace, putting on lipstick with care. She turned around as Katherine went in. 'Oh, good—it worked. Clever Henry! I'm off to the pub to have drinks with a few friends. You'll find food for the children in the fridge.'

'You're not ill,' said Katherine slowly.

Her sister-in-law turned on her in sudden fury. 'Of course I'm not—just bored to tears with nothing but the house and children and Mrs Todd away. Why shouldn't you have your share of cooking and cleaning?'

Katherine held on to her temper with an effort. 'I had my share,' she said quietly, 'and now I'm going straight back to my job.' But as she said it she heard the car door bang and Henry driving away. She said steadily, 'There is a bus in the late afternoon. I shall go back on that, and don't try and stop me, Joyce. Where are the children?'

Joyce shrugged. 'Upstairs, I suppose. Thank God they'll be going back to school in a few days—there has been 'flu or something, and they've had an extra week. I'm off.'

'You weren't going to leave the children on their own, were you?' asked Katherine.

'Of course not. Knew you'd come, you're a gullible little fool.' She laughed. 'What's known as a soft touch. And don't tell me you're going back now. Your pious conscience wouldn't allow you to do that, would it?'

Katherine turned on her heel and went upstairs. If she had stayed a moment longer, she would have thrown something at Joyce. She had no choice but to stay until she could get the bus just after five o'clock; she must make the best of it.

The children were strangely quiet in a nursery which sadly needed a good clean. She got them to wash their hands and faces, made their beds and tidied the room before going downstairs with them. Joyce had gone, and the kitchen bore evidence of her neglect. The breakfast things were still on the table, and the stove was a clutter of pots and pans.

'Hungry?' asked Katherine, and saw the children's faces light up. She gave them biscuits while she did a lightning clean up, opened cans and made toast and fed them, then settled them to play at the table. There was no sign of Joyce, so she loaded the washing machine and set it going, and then laid one end of the table for the children's tea. The afternoon was waning, and she saw with something like despair the clock hands creeping round to five. There was still no Joyce when she heard the bus go lumbering past.

It was almost an hour later, as the children were finishing their tea, that Joyce came back. She stood in the doorway, laughing. 'Missed the bus?' she wanted to know. 'Now you'll have to stay the night, won't you? And don't expect Henry to drive you back, he's going to some meeting or other, and won't be back until late.' She came further into the kitchen. 'The children have had their tea? Good. I'm very tired, perhaps you'll see them into their beds.' She yawned. 'I think I'll have a really early night myself. Get yourself some supper, and you might bring me up something later on.'

'I'll do no such thing. The children can't cook for themselves, but you can, Joyce.' Katherine turned her back and started to clear the table, and after a moment Joyce went away.

Katherine started to wash the dishes. She longed to

drop everything, but how could she? The children were tiresome, ill-behaved and ungrateful, but they were children and needed looking after. She sniffed away threatening tears and stacked the plates with unnecessary violence and a good deal of noise. Which was why she didn't hear the front door bell, nor the voices in the hall. When the kitchen door opened and she turned round to see what Joyce wanted, she saw Jason standing there.

She flung the dishmop into the sink and flew across the kitchen.

'Jason! Oh, Jason, please take me away!' She caught at his coat sleeves with soapy hands, and snivelled into his rock-solid chest. 'The bus went, and I thought I'd have to stay here for ever, and Joyce isn't ill at all—and Henry went away again before I could stop him.' She lifted her head to look at him. 'So sorry,' she said politely, and sniffed mournfully. She would have taken her hands away, but he caught and held them.

'I thought you might be here,' he said calmly. 'Get your coat, Katie.'

Joyce was standing in the doorway, watching them. Katherine brushed past her, put on her coat and found her handbag. 'There's a load of washing in the machine,' she said and added, 'Goodbye, children.'

They scarcely looked up, and Joyce said shrilly, 'You can't go! I'm ill...' But she didn't say any more, for the doctor was looking at her with a detached interest which made nonsense of the words.

He wished her goodnight civilly, nodded to the

children and ushered Katherine into the hall and out of the door. As they went down the path, he said casually, 'Sorry I couldn't come sooner. I had out-patients.'

He didn't say any more, and Katherine, unable to think of anything in reply, didn't answer.

CHAPTER NINE

JASON didn't speak again, and it wasn't until he had left Wilton behind and was driving slowly through the outskirts of Salisbury that Katherine said hesitantly, 'If you would put me down by the station, I can walk through to Mrs Potts…and thank you very much for coming for me. How did you know?'

'Your friend Andy.'

'Oh!' She said worriedly, 'Perhaps I shouldn't have left the children—perhaps Joyce *is* ill and didn't want to say so…'

He gave a crack of laughter. 'There's nothing wrong with your sister-in-law, take my word for it. She is perfectly able to look after her own children.'

'Here's the station…'

'So it is.' He swept past it. 'I dare say you had no lunch worth speaking of. I didn't either. We'll see what Mrs Spooner has for us.'

She murmured half-heartedly, and he took not the least bit of notice, but drove through the city until they reached the close and his house. 'I don't think…' began Katherine, making no attempt to get out of the car.

For answer, he undid her seat-belt, got out of the car and came round to open her door. When she got out, very reluctantly, he marched her into the house, all without saying a word.

Once inside, he said, 'Let me have your coat. Ah, here is Mrs Spooner. I expect you want to do your hair, or something of the sort. I'll be in the sitting-room.' He walked away with the dogs crowding round him, and she followed Mrs Spooner to the cloakroom. Once ushered inside, she did her best with her hair and face. She saw her reflection with horror in the looking-glass; it was pale and tear-stained and faintly grubby, and her hair was a mess. She looked a little better when she had finished, but not much, and a faint colour washed over her cheeks as she entered the sitting-room and encountered the doctor's thoughtful stare.

'Come and sit down. There will be a meal presently. In the meanwhile, have a glass of sherry and tell me exactly how your brother managed to get you away from your work.'

She explained in her sensible way, keeping strictly to the facts of it and making no bid for his sympathy. 'I'm sorry I behaved so stupidly when you came,' she finished. 'I was so very glad to see you.'

He said lightly, 'Well, you know the hospital isn't so well staffed that we can afford to lose even one nursing aide.'

A remark which reminded her who he was and who she was too, and uttered in so friendly a voice that she was unable to take umbrage, although it hurt. She said woodenly, 'Well, I'm on duty tomorrow, and I was only away for a few hours. Should I go and see Matron in the morning?'

'I think it might be the right thing to do.' He got up as Mrs Spooner came to say that the soup was on the table. As they sat down, he said easily, 'Edward is coming next weekend. I dare say he will want to see something of you.'

'Well, I'm supposed to be working long days on Saturday and on Sunday, so I don't think that will be possible.'

'A pity. He likes you. Do you like him, Katie?'

She spooned the last of her soup. 'Oh, yes! He'd be a marvellous brother—but you know that, I can remember telling you.'

'I have a shocking memory,' observed the doctor mendaciously. 'I have to recommend this sole. Have some, will you? Mrs Spooner is a marvellous cook.'

The sole was followed by apple pie and cream. Katherine, who had been quite famished, had a second helping at the doctor's gentle insistence before they went back to the sitting-room for their coffee.

She sighed with pleasure as she poured it; the gadrooned silver coffee-pot, the delicate china cups, set out exactly so on the snowy lace-edged cloth, the little dish of chocolate mints, all added up to an understated elegance which reminded her of her parents' home, a life-style seeming to her to be part of another world, never to be repeated.

She passed Jason his cup and saucer and, since the silence had gone on too long, said, 'You've been very kind, I really am most grateful.'

He smiled a little and sat back in his chair, drinking his coffee, while she sought anxiously for something to say. It was of no use; all she could think of was the fact that she was hopelessly in love with him. She put down her cup, annoyed that her hand shook so that it rattled in the saucer. 'If you don't mind,' she said with a kind of polite desperation, 'I think I had better go.'

The doctor made no move. 'Running away, Katie?' he asked blandly.

It was really too much. 'Yes, if you must know, I am.'

'Am I to know why?'

She studied his face. He knew; she felt cold at the thought, and then went very red. 'You know already.' She got up and started towards the door, but he was there before her, his arms holding her close. She stared up into his face; he wasn't smiling, indeed, he looked almost stern.

'Will you marry me, Katie? This isn't the first time I've asked this question, is it, and you've never quite believed me, have you? But you can't deny your love for ever.'

She said steadily, 'No—but there's Dodie…'

'Shall we forget about Dodie? I have asked you to marry me, Katie. I believe that you love me, perhaps not very much as yet, but love grows if you let it.'

She wanted to tell him that she already loved him so much that it had engulfed her whole life, but she stopped herself in time. She said soberly, 'Well, yes,

I think I do love you, Jason, but I don't know you very well, if you see what I mean.'

He laughed a little. 'We'll have to remedy that. I'll not hurry you, my dear. Just get used to the idea of marrying me in the not too distant future.' He bent his head and kissed her gently. 'Now I'm going to take you back to Mrs Potts.'

During the short drive he talked trivialities, opened the door for her, kissed her again, just as gently, and waited while she went indoors. Standing in the little hall, she reflected that he had said nothing about seeing her again, and took comfort from the fact that he wasn't given to unnecessary talk. Of course he would see her again.

She bade Mrs Potts goodnight without going into the kitchen, and went upstairs to her room, where she sat down on the bed and collected her excited thoughts. It was all her dreams come true, and so— she sought for the word—quietly. She had always imagined that a proposal would be thrilling and exciting, but she hadn't felt either thrilled or excited, only wonderment that it had happened to her, and a great wave of happiness. She went over the whole thing, every word he had uttered, her own words, too. It was while she was undressing that the thought struck her that he hadn't said that he loved her. She worried around the thought for some time, to come to the conclusion that since he wanted to marry her he must naturally love her, too. She got into bed and lay imagining a blissful future until she slept.

It was a dark, wet morning when she got up, but

she didn't care about that. Nothing could damp the happiness. She dressed, breakfasted and went out into the miserable morning. The hospital was already in the throes of early-morning busyness, with breakfast trolleys being wheeled through the wards, night staff going off duty and day staff picking up the reins of the ward routine, curtains round the beds of those for operation that morning, and Andy, already there, making up a bed for an emergency admission. She greeted Katherine with her usual good nature, declared that she was delighted to see her back so quickly, and wanted to know what had come over her. 'You look as though you'd won the pools or got yourself a millionaire.'

Katherine smiled widely, but before she could reply one of the senior student nurses came bustling along to tell them importantly to start making beds as soon as possible. 'All right, love,' said the irrepressible Andy, 'keep your hair on! We're women, not machines.'

They began making beds, starting on the other side of the ward, where most of the patients were in a state to help themselves a little, well enough to read the papers and joke with their neighbours and the nurses. It was while they were making their third bed that the occupant, an elderly man who had lived in Salisbury all his life and professed to knowing everyone and everything there, remarked that there would be a grand wedding before long.

'How come?' asked Andy. 'Anyone we know?'

He took the local paper off his locker and opened

it and handed it to her. 'Miss Dodie Grainger,' he told them importantly, 'well-known local upper-crust beauty, as you might say, got herself engaged to Sir Gerald Wilden—he's got a big estate between here and Chippenham—pots of money, too. Done well for herself, she has. I bet she broke a few hearts, too.'

Andy was reading the paper, and when she'd finished she offered it to Katherine, but the sight of Katherine's pale face made her put the paper down. 'I say, love, what's up? Do you feel sick? You look awful. You're not going to faint?'

Katherine forced a voice from a throat gone suddenly dry... 'No, I'm quite all right. It's just that it's warm in here, and it was so cold coming to work, and I didn't have much time for breakfast.' She managed a smile. 'I feel better already.' She smoothed the counterpane, a small, wan ghost of her usual self.

They went steadily down the row of beds, and she listened to Andy's cheerful chatter and answered it mechanically while her unhappy thoughts raced to and fro inside her head. At least she had told no one. Thank heaven for that! She had been a fool, blinded by love, willing to be bamboozled into declaring it, too. Jason had known that; she had been so easily convinced because she had wanted to be. It was as plain as the nose on her face now; Dodie had rejected him for another man, and he wanted to show her that he did not care, even though it must have been a cruel blow to him. What better than to find another girl to marry; show Dodie that he could be happy without her. Only, of course, he *wouldn't* be happy.

She went steadily about her work, only half aware of what she was doing. It was a mercy she was off duty earlier than usual, she would go to her room and get it sorted out for, of course, something would have to be done. She would have to see Jason and tell him that in no way would she consider marrying him. Only not today, she prayed silently. And had her prayers answered when she overheard Sister telling the house physician that it would be no good referring one of the patients to Dr Fitzroy's clinic, because he had gone to Southampton for several days.

The news brought Katherine a respite; at least there was no danger of her meeting him in the hospital, and by the time he returned she would be able to present a cool, level-headed front. Suddenly unwilling to be on her own in her room, she had a coffee at the hospital, and walked home through the main streets, stopping to look at the shop windows without really seeing anything in them.

When she at length got to Mrs Potts' house, she lingered in the kitchen, talking to that lady, to regret it before long when Mrs Potts remarked, 'I see our Miss Dodie has got herself engaged. I always thought she'd set her cap at Dr Fitzroy. I'm sure it was expected, not that he ever did say anything, although she was always hinting.'

Katherine mumbled, 'Oh, really? Well, I must get my letters written...'

'You look tired, love. There's a nice steak and kidney pudding for supper. Mind you come down for it, it'll put a bit of colour in your cheeks.'

Katherine made tea and then sat by the gas fire, drinking it, but it didn't warm the icy coldness lying like a lump in her chest. She would have to pull herself together. There was bound to be talk about the engagement at supper; after all, Dodie, although not known personally, was known to Mrs Potts through the titbits of gossip she had from Mrs Spooner. When Mrs Potts rang the bell for supper, she went downstairs, nicely in command of herself. It was most fortunate that Miss Fish had witnessed a small street accident that afternoon and insisted on recounting it in much detail, so that most of the meal was eaten to her recital; they were eating their pudding before Mrs Potts mentioned Dodie's engagement, and Katherine was able to utter suitable exclamations to the various opinions of the subject. She was even able to agree that Dodie was a remarkably pretty young woman and would be a beautiful bride.

'All the same,' observed Mrs Potts as they prepared to leave the table, 'I quite thought she'd have Dr Fitzroy.'

'Perhaps he didn't ask her,' said Miss Fish in her dry, elderly voice.

'Why, he's been taking her around for I don't know how long,' protested Mrs Potts, 'and she so free and easy with him, so my sister told me.'

Back in her room, Katherine got out the sweater she was knitting and went doggedly to work on its complicated pattern. Of course, since she wasn't concentrating, the pattern became a nightmare; she was unpicking it when there was a knock on the door. It was probably Shirley, come to borrow tea or sugar, for she never seemed to have any of her own. Katherine called 'come in,' and looked up to see Jason standing in the doorway.

'You're in Southampt n!' she gasped, and then, 'Oh, Jason, go away.'

He stayed where he was, eyeing her narrowly. 'I've only just got here,' he pointed out reasonably. 'What's wrong, Katie?'

Despite her best efforts, her voice was shrill. 'Wrong? Everything is.' Her feelings were rapidly getting the better of her. 'Did you know that Dodie was going to get married?'

'Of course.'

'So, to get even because she wouldn't marry you, you wanted to show her that it didn't matter, by marrying someone yourself—me, and what could be easier?' She had stood up, and now she stamped her foot with rage. 'I could die of shame telling you that I loved you...'

He said quietly, 'Will you sit down so that we can talk sensibly?'

'No, I will not. I'm not in the mood to be sensible...'

His face was as calm as it always was, but she sensed anger behind the calm. 'No, I can see that. I'll go, and when you have simmered down and rid yourself of all this nonsense you can come and tell me.'

The anger showed now, although it was tightly controlled. He hadn't moved an inch, but she took a step backwards, something which made him give a short laugh. 'I came racing back from Southampton to be with you, and what do I find? A termagant with her head full of rubbishy fancies.'

'I'm not a ter—termagant...' She wasn't exactly sure what that was, but it sounded unpleasant.

He enlightened her: 'A vixen, a virago, a battle-axe.' He paused, smiling in a manner to chill her heart. 'No, not a battle-axe, you haven't the shape.'

Katherine drew an indignant breath. 'Go away! I never want to see you again.' And then, because she loved him so much, 'I'm sorry if Dodie has broken your heart, but you need not have broken mine, too.'

He looked at her without expression. 'You know where I am when you want me, Katie.' He had gone, leaving her with her mouth open, ready to deny that she would ever need to speak to him again.

She had a good cry after that, and then sat, her face blotched and her eyelids swollen, and reviewed his visit. Perhaps she should have allowed him to talk as he had wanted to, but she had been upset and very angry. She still was, but the light of reason was creeping in, and she had to admit that perhaps she had been over-hasty, and certainly undignified. She should have been sweetly reasonable, allowed him to make his excuses and then quietly pointed out that she had no wish to marry him. She supposed that only heroines in novels ever did this, but she wasn't in a book, she was flesh and blood and hurt and humiliated, and very much in love, even though she no longer *liked* Jason. She amended this: she didn't like him at the moment.

She got up and made a pot of tea and got ready for

bed. There was no point in reiterating her sad thoughts. She got into bed and closed her eyes, but stayed awake until it was almost time to get up.

She was getting ready to go out and shop when Mrs Potts called up the stairs to say that there was a telephone call for her. Her heart leapt; Jason wanted to see her again, despite his unkind remarks about her going to see him. She raced down to the hall and lifted the receiver.

It was Mrs Grainger. 'We're back for a time, dear,' explained the old lady. 'We've been very happy with Tom, but we wanted to come home and see all our friends again. Dodie has found us a very pleasant companion. We would like to see you—could you come to tea one day soon? Tomorrow, perhaps?'

Katherine had no reason not to go, so she agreed to call in on her way home the following afternoon and said goodbye. It was only after she had rung off that she wondered how Mrs Grainger had known where she was. She dismissed the thought, and went back upstairs to get her small shopping list and her purse.

She didn't see Jason that day, but she hadn't expected to, for he had returned to Southampton; she overheard Sister telling the house surgeon that he wouldn't be back until the end of the week. Longing to see him, but determined not to, Katherine went about her work and, when she got back to Mrs Potts' that evening, had her supper and went straight to bed with the plea of a headache.

She had her lunch at the hospital the next day, after

she had been on duty for a half-day, so it was well after two o'clock by the time she reached the Graingers' house. Mrs Dowling opened the door to her.

'Well, now, it's a treat to see you again,' she declared, relaxing her stern features into a smile. 'You've filled out nicely, too, though you're a bit pale. Hard work, I've no doubt! Come on in, they're waiting for you. I'll be bringing in the tea a bit early. That new companion's got the afternoon off...' And, at Katherine's enquiring look, 'She's all right, but she doesn't give a hand like you used to.'

Katherine was led through the familiar hall and ushered into the drawing-room, where Mr and Mrs Grainger were sitting in their usual places on each side of the fire.

They greeted her warmly, and Mrs Grainger launched at once into a rather muddled account of their stay with Tom Fetter. It had been very pleasant, she conceded, but it seemed that his household was a very expensive one to maintain. 'For, of course, Mr Grainger considered it necessary to share any expenses while we were there. But, really, it seemed prudent to return here, for we live very simply ourselves at very much less cost.'

Katherine murmured sympathetically; the Graingers were obviously not lacking in the world's goods, and Mrs Grainger's ideas of living simply were hardly hers; Tom had very likely been getting money from them on one pretext or another, and old Mr Grainger was no fool.

Mrs Grainger, having exhausted Tom Fetter and his house as a topic of conversation, started off again.

'You will have heard about our dear Dodie; the dear girl…done very well for herself, too. She will have a splendid wedding, of course. We always thought that she would marry Dr Fitzroy, but strangely enough he never fell in love with her, although all the other young men did.'

Mrs Grainger turned her gentle face towards Katherine. 'He was always so kind, too, taking her here and there, putting up with her little tantrums, but he treated her like a young sister.' She laughed a little. 'It annoyed Dodie, of course, she liked to think that she could twist any man she knew round her little finger. He's away, you know, but we hope to see him when he gets back. I dare say you see something of him at the hospital?'

Katherine said in a careful, matter-of-fact voice, 'Well, no, very seldom. He is a consultant physician and I'm just a nursing aide on the surgical ward. How did you know where I was, Mrs Grainger?'

It was Mr Grainger who answered her. 'Mrs Dowling told us, and it wasn't all that hard to get hold of you, my dear. You're happy at the hospital?'

'Very happy, and I have a most comfortable room…'

She cast about for something to talk about, and was about to fall back on the weather when Mrs Dowling came in with the tea things, and the little flurry of pouring out, passing cups and offering cakes, made it unnecessary to do more than talk trivialities. Which

was a good thing, for she was mulling over what Mrs
Grainger had said about Jason and Dodie. If it were
true, and there was no reason to believe that Mrs
Grainger would tell fibs, then she would have to seek
out Jason and apologise. The idea appalled her, and
she was thankful that for the next few days he would
be away; by the time he returned, she would have
decided on what to say, and, what was more important, where. Somewhere she could escape from
quickly. She had days off at the end of the week, and
the best thing to do would be to go to his house as
she came off duty the evening before and then go
away for her days off. She had been saving her wages
for a jersey suit, and there was enough money to pay
for bed and breakfast in some small hotel. Even if he
wanted to see her, and she very much doubted that,
he would give up after two days, and at the end of
that time, she thought hopefully, she would be able
to face him if she had to.

She collected her wandering thoughts and made a
vague reply to Mr Grainger's enquiries as to her
work. Presently, with the promise that she would
come again, she took herself off.

She spent a wretched night, reminding herself of
all the things she had said to Jason. She had told him
to go away and, what was more, he had done just
that, without a backward glance. She burst into tears
at the thought. Well, he would see now how little it
mattered to her; she would leave the hospital and go
miles away and be very successful at something or
other—she had no idea what at the moment. She sat

up in bed, sniffing and snivelling at the very idea, trying to bring some sense to her unhappy thoughts.

The week went by. If Jason was back, she saw nothing of him and, by the time she was ready to go off duty before her days off, she had convinced herself that he hadn't yet returned. So much the better, she told herself, the longer the time before they must inevitably meet, the better.

'I am, in fact, a coward,' she muttered, changing into her outdoor clothes in the cold cloakroom. He was still away, but she couldn't wait to scurry back to Mrs Potts', pack a case, and take herself off in the early morning, ostensibly to stay with an aunt, but in actual fact to spend her days off in Winchester. Shirley had mentioned casually that there was a small cheap hotel close to the bus station there, and she could spend her days at museums and the cathedral and go window shopping. At least she wouldn't see Jason.

She raced through the hospital, a bundle of nerves, and made for the main doors, to dart through them, straight into Jason's outstretched arms.

'Oh, dear!' said Katherine, aware as she said it that it was a silly, meaningless thing to say. Dodie would have had some witty quip ready on her tongue. She stood, held tight by his arms, staring speechlessly into his face. It told her nothing. She had never known a man, she reflected crossly, who could look so bland. 'I'm going away,' she said rather breathlessly. 'Days off, you know...'

'Yes, I know.' He smiled faintly. 'I thought you

might like to know that I'm back—just in case you might have something to say to me.'

'No—yes—no, I haven't.'

'Undecided? A little peace and quiet while you think it over?' He whisked her across the forecourt and into the Bentley, and was beside her, driving away, before she could utter a word.

'I should like to go home.'

'Well, I thought you might.' He was driving round the close, within moments they would be at his own front door.

'I shan't get out,' she spoke very loudly, to convince herself as well as him.

He drew up and turned to look at her. 'Listen to your heart, Katie, my darling girl, and listen to me telling you that I love you.'

'You're not fair!' She sucked in her breath like a child.

'No, I know that, but then, you're such a very stubborn girl. If you had listened to your heart in the first place, and not rushed helter-skelter into a whole maze of silly imaginings...'

'I'm not silly,' said Katherine peevishly.

'Yes, you are, but don't worry, I love you when you're silly, just as much as I love you when you're being fiercely practical.'

He got out, walked round to her side, opened the door and scooped her out. Standing on the pavement before his house, she found her voice.

'It's no use, I won't go in. I'm going away for my days off.' She added, 'But I intended coming to see you after that. I thought I'd be quite—quite sensible by then, you see. You said I'd know where to find you, and I'd have to see you again so that I could apologise—I didn't give you a chance to speak...'

Jason sorted out this speech apparently to his satisfaction. 'Well, since you're here, you might as well come inside and apologise handsomely.'

'No,' said Katherine. It cost quite a lot to say it.

'Well, my darling girl, if you prefer to stand out here in this biting wind, by all means do so. That is, if you don't mind going to the altar with a streaming cold.'

'The altar?'

'I've always fancied the idea of a really quiet wedding, just us and one or two friends. I'll get a licence tomorrow.'

She was conscious of two great arms enfolding her. They felt heavenly, but she said firmly, 'Dodie?'

'My dearest heart, neither Dodie nor any other woman who may have taken my passing fancy means anything to me. But you—the moment I saw you standing there in that old dressing-gown, looking like an earnest mouse with the most beautiful eyes in the world—I lost my heart, Katie, and you have held it in your hand ever since. I never knew that falling in love could be such a devastatingly sudden thing, or so fragile...I hardly dared breathe for fear you might take fright and scamper off.'

'Well, I had thought about doing that. You see, I thought that you and Dodie...'

'Plague take the girl! I love you, Katie, my darling. Will you marry me?'

She said dreamily, 'I fell in love with you in the canteen at the hospital. You'd told them to give me a good breakfast.'

His vast chest heaved with laughter. 'Oh, my darling girl!' He freed an arm and opened his door. 'Come home, my love.'

She held back for a moment. 'You really love me—want to marry me? It's not just a dream?'

'If you come inside, I'll do my best to convince you on both counts,' said Jason, and bent to kiss her.

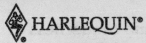

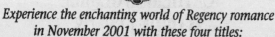

Three of your favorite authors will move you to tears
and laughter in three wonderfully emotional stories,
bringing you…

Mistletoe Miracles

A brand-new anthology from

BETTY NEELS
CATHERINE GEORGE
MARION LENNOX

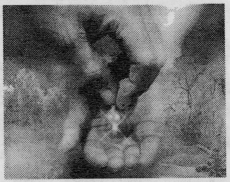

The warmth and magic of the holiday season comes alive
in this collection in which three couples learn that
Christmas is a time when miracles really *do* come true.

Available in November 2001 at your favorite retail outlet.

HARLEQUIN®
Makes any time special ®

Visit us at www.eHarlequin.com   PHMBC